Until I Needed the Song

The Story of That Time God and Jesus
Took an Angel Named Abigail
On a Road Trip

apocryphile press
BERKELEY, CA

Apocryphile Press
1700 Shattuck Ave #81
Berkeley, CA 94709
www.apocryphile.org

Printed in the United States of America
ISBN 9781940671765

Dedication

This book is dedicated to

MIKE YACONELLI

whose humor and faith still inspire me.

Acknowledgements

John Mabry: For bravery.

Paul: For the education about blue slurpees

Carl Reiner: His God shaped mine.

The Snapple Company: If Jesus drinks Baltic Blast maybe they will revive the flavor.

All the youth groups who have sat and listened to these stories in all their many forms.

Marjorie: Yeah, that one was you.

Tom Waits: You really haven't lived until you've driven down the highway at night with the windows open screaming along with Jersey Girl. His song "San Diego Serenade" inspired the title of this book.

Trader Joe's: Whose coffee was consumed in great quantites during the creation of this book.

Becky: For patience and love beyond all understanding.

Table of Contents

Introduction

First, thanks for getting this far. Hopefully you will finish the book. It may not be an easy read for some of you. Some may laugh. Some may tear up here and there. It is my hope that you will talk. Find a friend and discuss what you read over coffee. Start a book club. Give it as a gift. It should be more than shelf space or memory if you are reading on your favorite e-reader.

I first saw God when I was in kindergarten. Kindergarden Sunday school to be more precise. I'm sure I had a children's Bible. I'm sure my mother read me stories from it. But my first real memory of God came in that classroom. The teacher's name was Mrs. Mallot. She was a nice woman who cracked her gum and had eyebrows that were drawn on. She had a flannel board (a high point in Sunday school technology for many years). One Sunday she put a picture of God on the board. She said, "See? That's God."

It was classic Sunday School God, the Father Almighty, the Creator of Heaven and Earth. He was a white guy and he was really old. He sat on a big throne with a multitude of angels flitting about his head like gnats. He did not look happy. He looked constipated.

As time goes on and we grow up we are able to process all sorts of different images of who God is or what God is. Is God a great cosmic blob in the sky of wibbly-wobbly stuff or is God us and are we God and does God exist because we do? Did we make God in our image (thank you Jethro Tull) or is it the other way around?

Someone once told me that I worship a God with dirt under his fingernails. The image of God kneeling down in the dirt and breathing life into this lump of clay he fashioned has always been a powerful one. Or is God something else entirely? Is God a being who is so far beyond our understanding that Walt Disney, Steve Jobs, Henry Ford, and Leonardo Da Vinci could not conceive of all that God is if they sat around the table and talked about it deep into the night?

What if our senses—smell, sight, sound, taste and touch—what if those were limitations? What if when we shuffle off this mortal coil we are no longer limited by those senses? What if God is a being of unlimited senses? And we simply did not understand all that God is because God is beyond taste, touch, smell, sight and sound?

Or what if God is an old guy with a beard?

My attempt in this book was to write about that flannel-board God as seen through the eyes of an adult. What stories would we tell if we never reasoned out the whole "cosmic blob" thing? What if the God we worshipped is the God from the flannel board?

What if he and his son spent time playing basketball, or hung out with the saints at Heaven's Welcome Station? What if God took the occasional personal interest in one new arrival?

Prologue

Ring…

Ring…

Ring…

Suicide prevention.

This is the suicide prevention hot line. Is there someone there?

I can hear you. Do you want to tell me your name? Just your first name.

Abigail.

Abigail. Do people call you Abby?

Sometimes.

Which do you prefer?

Abby.

Abby. Okay. Abby, where are you?

Do I have to answer that? Do I have to tell you where I live?

No. I mean where are you, like in your house. Are you even in your own house?

I'm in my bedroom.

Is there anyone else in the house with you?

No.

Is there a friend you could call to come over and sit with you?

No.

Why did you call tonight?

I'm just having a really bad day.

Abby, have you taken any pills.

Not yet.

Do you have some there?

My mom's sleeping pills.

Would you be willing to put the pills in another room and then come back to your room so we can talk?

I don't think so.

Why not?

Because I don't want you to talk me out of this.

Then why did you call me?

So they would think I had second thoughts? They'll see it on the phone bill in a month or so.

Who is "they"? Your mom and dad?

Everybody.

Everybody?

Yes.

Why do you want them to think you had second thoughts?

So they'll think that maybe they could have done something.

That's awfully cruel, isn't it?

What do you mean?

I mean, why do you want to hurt them so much?

They won't miss me.

Nobody? There's nobody who will miss you?

Lots of things would just be better if I were to just disappear.

Why would you want to disappear?

I'm sick and tired of being sick and tired.

Are you sick?

No. That was something my grandmother used to say.

I see.

I just think it would make it a lot easier on everyone if I weren't around.

You don't think anyone would miss you?

My mom will wear it like a big bright pin. Everybody will look at her and say, "Oh, isn't she holding up well, the poor dear."

What about your dad?

What about him?

What will he do?

He won't even know I'm gone till he reads it in the paper.

That doesn't sound like you're hurting them.

I don't want to hurt them. I just want them to notice me.

They ignore you?

I'm the invisible girl.

Like in the comic books.

What?

The Invisible Girl in the comic books. She could disappear and nobody knew where she was. She could walk through walls and do anything. I've got some if you want to read them sometime.

I don't think so.

Why not?

I'm not going to be here.

I've got Superman, too.

Is this your first time answering the phones?

No. I've been doing this a few years now.

Ever lose anybody?

Sorry. Your turn.

Huh?

You know I've worked here for a few years and you know I like comic books. Now tell me something about you.

I'm 16 and I have pills.

You told me about the pills already. Tell me something else. Do you like sports?

No.

Music.

Not really.

Ben and Jerry's?

What flavor?

What's your favorite?

Double chocolate fudge with cookie dough and brownie chunks.

I like Mint Oreo. I've got some here at the center. Do you want to come in and have some?

I have some here at home.

You can't kill yourself if you have Ben and Jerry's in the freezer.

Is that a rule?

Of course it is.

You made it up.

No. It's a rule.

Is not. And you're not going to keep me on the phone by arguing.

What do you think will happen if you kill yourself?

My mom will be horribly embarrassed by the whole thing.

I mean to you.

I'll be dead.

And then?

That's it.

There's nothing else?

That's it.

You're sure?

Yes.

Tell me how you know.

I prayed and nothing happened.

That's it? That's how you know?

Yes.

What did you pray for?

You're not going to do this.

Do what?

Keep me on the phone till my parents get home.

When do they get home?

I don't know. Tomorrow sometime.

I got no place to go.

You have no life.

That's what my ex-girlfriend said.

You had a girlfriend?

Yes.

She dump you?

First you tell me about your boyfriend.

How did you know I had a boyfriend?

I've done this before.

You're trying to keep me on the phone again.

I'm trying to understand why you would want to kill yourself when you have Ben and Jerry's in the freezer.

Why do you care?

You sound like an interesting person. Even if you do have bizarre taste in ice cream.

It won't work.

The ice cream?

You can't keep me on the phone forever.

Like I said I have no place to go.

That's your problem.

Tell me one of yours.

Sorry. Won't work.

Abigail, why don't you get the Ben and Jerry's, flush the pills, and I'll tell you all about why my girlfriend left me.

I think I'm okay now. Thanks for talking with me.

Abigail—

Goodbye.

Abigail, don't hang up.

Chapter

(1)

The basketball court was an exact duplicate of the one in Madison Square Garden, right down to the pattern of the wood grain in the floorboards. Even the floor wax smelled the same. This is where they played sometimes. Not every time... but sometimes. Sometimes the court was a ragged blacktop with nets made out of chains. You could find one like it on the public playground in Chicago. Sometimes they liked to play on the court from the high school in Milan, Indiana. A very old court in a very old school with proper squeaky floors and old wooden bleachers. This one looked like Madison Square Garden.

There was, however, no ceiling. The walls on all four sides of the gym just seemed to continue past any point where a ceiling full of lights should be. There were no seats. This was not a court for spectators. Clouds often formed at the top and it occasionally rained. Having no ceiling, the court opened onto a sea of stars that no human being had ever seen.

The ball slammed hard against the side wall. The sound went straight up and echoed off the upper regions of the gym. The echo returning down sounded like thunder to the two men playing one-on-one but neither gave the sound a second thought.

They played hard. Throwing themselves down the court and back again. Both had long hair pulled back into ponytails. Both were bearded. The elder's hair and beard were white as wedding cake frosting. The younger's, brown, with deep brown eyes. His skin was like coffee and cream from a lifetime in the sun. Despite their differences even the most casual observer could see immediately that these two were father and son. The most casual observer, being in a place to see them together, would already know they were Father and Son.

The Father, currently in possession of the ball, threw himself down the court huffy and sweaty. The Son followed so close he was practically riding his father's back. God stopped short in the center of the court. Jesus slammed into him from behind and fell backward to the floor. God did not turn around. He took his sweet time and set a long half-court shot that sailed through the air gracefully and then bounced off the rim with a loud "Ba-WAAAAAANG" and off to the left where it hit the wall and then dropped to the floor. The ball bounced twice. The second was higher than the first. On the third bounce the ball lighted on the orange rim where it circled the net four times before simply dropping through.

God turned back toward Jesus, who was still sitting on the floor panting. God smiled. Jesus said, "Are you going to play basketball or are you going to screw around?"

"You were crowding," God said.

"I wasn't. You were moving too slow and I was getting ready to run over you." Jesus wiped the sweat from his forehead with the back of his sweaty arm. God reached out his hand and helped the Savior to his feet. "That doesn't count."

"Fine, have it your way, Mama's Boy," God said, smiling.

"Omnipotent," Jesus said.

"Emmanuel," God retorted.

"Yahweh."

"Rabboni."

"Look, we both know I can do this longer. You have more names."

"Show off," God said.

The ball had found a spot by the wall and stopped. Now it suddenly rolled across the floor by itself and, just before hitting the toe of his Converse, popped into the air and into Jesus hands. Jesus looked at his father. "I said quit that."

"Take it out," God said.

"Are you going to play straight?"

God nodded and motioned with his hands to start. Jesus took one step, bounced the ball, and spun to his left. He pushed the ball with both hands into the air where it sailed and dropped into the hoop. Nothing but net.

God stared at his son. There was no arguing. They both knew it was a fair shot. A little grandiose, possibly, but a fair shot nonetheless.

"Twenty," Jesus said.

"Again?" God asked.

"Just because you can beat Gabriel doesn't mean you can beat me."

"Gabriel lets me win."

"You're kidding."

God shook his head.

They walked toward the wall where a large red Igloo cooler was tucked into a corner. "You want tea?" God asked.

"Got Snappple?"

"You want that Baltic Blast stuff?"

"They don't make that anymore."

God looked at his son and raised an eyebrow.

"Baltic Blast would be nice."

God reached into the icy cooler and came up with a glass bottle and blindly tossed it over his shoulder. It dropped into the savior's hand. God pulled a tea out for himself and grabbed a towel from the floor. He wiped the sweat from his face and head and then sat down leaning against the wall.

"Ohhhhhhhhhhh me!" He said, and held the cold bottle to his forehead.

Jesus sat next to him, and they were both quiet for a moment.

"Basketball is a beautiful game," God said, "played with the legs and the tips of the fingers...."

"...demanding you to be a horse, but also a bird," Jesus finished. "I remember that from someplace. Who said it?"

"Keillor, I think," God said. "Might have been Magic."

"Sounds like Keillor," Jesus said, and opened his drink. He took a long pull at the bottle and then said, "So, Gabriel lets you win?"

God sighed and leaned his head back against the wall. He closed his eyes and a breeze seemed to drift down from the nonexistent ceiling. "Gabriel starts running away with the game and then he sees me huffing and puffing and he starts to make really stupid mistakes on purpose."

"He really thinks you don't know?"

"You can shut some things off, but not others. You and I, we play it straight. But once I read Gabriel to see what he was thinking."

"What did you find out?"

"I found out that he was letting me win."

"And what did we learn from this?" Jesus asked the question like a kindergarten Sunday school teacher.

God opened one eye and looked at Jesus.

"So," Jesus continued. "You found out that he was letting you win and then you *let* him let you win?"

"I also found out that it made him happy."

"You are a strange individual."

"You take after your mother," God returned.

The basketball in the corner of the room suddenly began to roll on its own. It made a long wide curve around the center of the court and rolled over to where the two men were sitting. God set down his tea and picked up the ball, spinning it on his finger.

A few swipes with his other hand and the ball was now spinning all on its own.

Jesus watched as the ball became a globe. Clay at first, dark and brown, but then it began to glow as if it were red hot. Clouds formed and rained down on the spinning, freshly-made planet. Jesus watched as the oceans began filling in. Beaches and land masses formed. The entire evolution of a planet spinning on the end of God's finger. In seconds they watched cities form. Highways shot across the land masses. Tiny planes and boats spanned the spaces between the land masses. Jesus watched as a rocket fired and hovered six inches above the spinning globe. He wanted to reach out and touch it, but knew he should not. The rocket returned to the planet and within a minute the land masses began firing missiles at each other. One side began to glow and then the other until the entire globe was once again hot and fiery. It cooled to black and gray and all the while continued to spin on the end of God's finger. It spun for another ten seconds before becoming a basketball again. God rolled the ball across the floor in disgust.

"Shoot," he said.

"A lot of them seem to end that way," Jesus said.

"They can cherish each other or they can kill each other. Their choice." God sipped his tea.

"Thanks for not sending me down again."

"I told you I wouldn't do that ever again. Never *that* way, at least. If you ever want to go back it's up to you."

"I'll think about it," Jesus said. He finished off the last of his bottle and set the empty by the cooler. "Another game? I'll spot you ten."

God shook his head.

"Your Majesty?"

Both the Father and the Son looked up as a young woman with red hair lowered herself out of the mist above. Her wings were fluffy and thick with large feathers. Her sparkling white robe hung past her feet, but that was okay because she hovered 12 inches from the floor. She looked like a child who had just been cast as the "main angel" in the Christmas pageant and had an overzealous mother.

God smiled and stood up. "Hello Abigail. Getting the hang of the new wings, I see."

The young angel did not look up from the floor, but Jesus could tell she was smiling. God took the angel's hand and kissed it in a very grandfatherly way. "What can I do for you, my dear?"

"St. Peter says he needs some help in the Welcome Station. There's a woman who wants to complain."

God looked at his son, who looked back. They both turned toward the young angel.

"She wants to what?" Jesus asked, trying not to laugh.

"She wants to talk to whomever is in charge," Abby said. "So Saint Peter asked me to come and get you."

"You can call him Pete," God said. "We're pretty informal around here."

"One thing at a time," Abby said. "Can I tell him you're on your way?"

"We'll be there in a jiffy," God said. He pointed toward the red cooler. "Would you like something before you go?"

"Got a Strawberry Yoo Hoo?" the angel asked.

"For you? Of course." God reached into the cooler and brought out a frosty bottle. The young angel took it and rose up, disappearing into the mist.

"Well," God said, "do you want to come along?"

"Sure," Jesus answered. "This might be interesting."

The two men walked out of a door that hadn't been there a minute ago. A second later the high walls, baskets, and cooler were gone too.

Chapter

2

Few people know this...well, few *living* people know this...but the Welcome Station in Heaven is nearly identical to the one in Jacksonville, Florida in the early 70's. During his many trips across the planet he created, God spent a great deal of time at the beach. He would often stand on the beach and breathe as the water lapped at his toes. It was the same thing he did on the day he created the heavens and the earth. The beach, being one of his favorite ideas at the time, held a special place in his heart. So he spent a lot of time there. There was something about the Jacksonville Welcome to Florida rest stop that made him smile every time he went.

There were free cups of fresh Florida orange juice and racks with dozens and dozens of brochures advertising fun things to see and do in the Sunshine State. Even if you had no intention of doing any of these things, they were fun to take and read in the car.

Jesus knew if they stopped in Jacksonville on the way to the beach he'd be driving the rest of the way while his father read interesting bits of trivia aloud from the Ripley's Believe it or Not Museum or Gatorland. Once God had suggested the giant gator mouth entrance to the alligator theme park be used in heaven.

"Not sure that's the first impression you want to make," Jesus had said.

"Good," God said. "Give 'em a jolt. Make 'em feel a little more appreciative when they realize it's heaven."

"Might be scary for the kids," the Son of Man suggested.

"We'll paint it pastel pink."

Such were the conversations God and Jesus had when they went to the beach.

God enjoyed the Welcome Station so much he decided that was the look he wanted for new arrivals.

The line was not too long today. It barely stretched out the door. It really wasn't an efficient system, but Peter had discovered that despite their religious beliefs on earth, people seemed to like the idea of a line and a man sitting on a stool with a giant book filled with names.

God wore his favorite Hawaiian shirt (the one with the martini cocktail glasses) and cargo shorts. Jesus wore one of his many Amy Grant concert T-shirts and jeans. "Do you want me in the whole white robe and cloak?" Jesus asked.

"Nah," his father said. "Let's just see how this plays out."

The Father and the Son walked through the back door (often referred to as the "servants' entrance") and found St. Peter sitting on a stool with the giant Book of Life open in front of him. Next to the book sat a small unassuming black box with a rather large intimidating red button. The side of the box read "Trap Door." It wasn't actually connected to anything. Jesus had made it as a joke for Peter, who seemed to get a kick out of the expression on people's faces as they looked from the book to the button and sweated.

Peter looked up and briefly waved at the pair and then motioned with his head toward the lobby.

The walls of the Welcome Station were glass and each opened out onto a different sort of vista. You could look out one wall and see snow-covered mountains and see serene beaches out another. These landscapes changed as if they were a slideshow, but if you looked hard enough you could see they weren't slides at all. The lobby was filled with blue vinyl-covered sofas with pink and orange pastel lamps on end tables. People who had been through the line milled about the lobby studying brochures and drinking the best orange juice they ever tasted. It was all intended to have a calming you're-on-vacation effect, but still some people looked around as if they had taken the wrong exit.

Off to one side with her back to the window a woman sat. Her body language screamed "don't touch me" so loud arriving people just automatically seemed to give her her own space. No one sat on the large sofa with her.

God and Jesus strolled over to where she was sitting. "Mrs. Blair?" God said. She stood when she saw them coming, as though she had been sitting on a spring.

"I want to talk with you," Thelma Blair said before the Creator of the Universe had finished saying her name. She looked at Jesus in his concert T-shirt and scowled. "Are you really the Son of God?"

She didn't say it as a woman who had spent her adult life teaching Sunday school. She said it as if she thought perhaps he should get a haircut.

"Yes," Jesus said. He held out his arms so she could see the scars on his wrists. "See?"

God said, "I understand you have some concerns."

"I don't have concerns," she said. Her words tightened the air around them. "I have a complaint."

"Well, we don't get many of those," God said, "but I can try to help out. What seems to be the problem?"

"I just saw my husband," she said. "I was on that tram tour and we passed over a huge city and I saw my husband. He was sitting outside of some sort of coffeehouse reading a newspaper. A newspaper, for crying out loud!"

God and Jesus were both silent for a moment. They looked at each other and then back at the small woman in front of them.

"He's not supposed to be here!" She said it as if they were missing the obvious.

"Oh," God said. He nodded as if it made sense and then looked at her quizzically. "Why not?"

She looked as shocked as if he was a child who had somehow

managed to leave his shoes in a public bathroom. "Because," she said. "He's a violent man. He used to beat me. Shove me against the wall and choke me. One time he broke my nose and told me to lie for him at the emergency room. Said he'd do worse if I told them what happened. Happiest day of my life is when he walked out in front of a truck. I only wish I had been there to see it. No, I wish I had been the one driving the truck."

God stood quietly and let her finish. He did not interrupt. He had arrived thinking the woman was being rude, but realized she was so filled with pain and bitterness she had not allowed herself any other emotions for years...the majority of her life. Her voice was on the edge. It quivered slightly, but she controlled it, reined it back in with her anger.

"Thelma," God said, his voice filled with love and empathy. "I know your husband. I was here when he came up. He is supposed to be here. Just as you are. Just as everyone is. This is a very big place. You don't have to see him if you don't want to."

"I don't care if I don't have to see him. I don't want him here *at all*. He doesn't deserve it. He should be rotting in hell. That's the only thing that's given me any comfort for the last 40 years; and now you tell me he's been here all along?" The coldness of her voice carried throughout the Welcome Station. People in the line outside pulled themselves a little closer.

"Your husband asked me to forgive him," God said. "I did."

"That's it?" she said incredulously.

"That's it."

"He was lying," Thelma Blair said.

"Do you think I wouldn't know if he was lying?"

She stopped. For a moment Jesus thought she was going to say "yes," but she kept it inside. She stood silently, her body trembling. She allowed a single tear to appear in one eye and then the walls she had built up for so many years began to crumble.

She lost her balance and nearly fell forward. Jesus caught her and she began to weep into his shoulder. "It's not fair," she sobbed. "It's just not fair."

God reached out and touched her on her back. "Yes, it is," he said. "It's completely fair. I gave everybody the opportunity to make choices. He made some bad ones, but so have you, Thelma."

Thelma Blair looked up when the Lord called her by her first name.

"You've spent so many years being so angry," God said. "There were so many people you pushed away because you were afraid to be hurt again."

"He made me this way," Thelma said.

"No," God said. "You did. There was so much bitterness in you that no one could get close. You pushed them away. They never got a chance to love you. Your husband was the same way. He was filled with anger and pain. I took all that away from him and he came to live here."

"I hate him," Thelma said.

"I know," said God. "But I can take the pain and the anger away if you will just give them to me. You can't bring them in with you."

Thelma pushed herself away from the Son of God. She wiped her tears away so hard she left marks on her own cheeks. Her anger had returned. "Are you saying that my wife-beating husband got into heaven after all he did to me?"

"It's called forgiveness," God said quietly.

Jesus straightened his T-shirt and looked at her. He could feel her start to stiffen even though she stood two feet from him.

"And if I choose not to forgive him—if I decide to hate him for what he did, then I can't come in?"

God looked very intently at her. "If you can't forgive him, Thelma, you can't forgive me. If you hate him, you hate me. It is one of the basic rules."

Thelma walked between the Father and the Son and strolled over to the large picture window. It looked out onto a huge open spacescape. She stood silently at the window for a while and then sat quietly in a vinyl-covered chair and said nothing.

God and Jesus waited a moment. Finally Jesus walked over and put his hand on her shoulder. She stiffened even more at his touch.

"Whenever you are ready," he said. "You have lots of time. Give me all the anger and bitterness and guilt. I know what to do with them. I'll fill in that empty space with grace and love. You'll see."

Thelma Blair did not move. She sat back on the sofa with her feet planted firmly on the floor. She clutched her purse in her lap as if she were afraid someone might come along and snatch it from her.

"Whenever you are ready," God said. Father and Son walked back over to where St. Peter was checking names.

"Need a break?" Jesus called.

"Absolutely," Peter said. "You want some coffee?"

"That'd be great," Jesus said. Peter then turned to God.

"Tea would be nice," God said.

Peter looked up and scanned the empty ceiling. "Abigail!" he called. The young red-headed angel lowered herself down as if she had been hovering over the Saint's desk the whole time. The people in line said, "Ooooooooooooo." Abigail smiled.

Peter said, "Find Paul and see if he can come and fill in for me for a bit."

Abigail lifted and then disappeared. Peter took a handmade, well-worn cardboard sign from beneath his desk. It read, "Back in five minutes" written in a script that would have made the most patient of monks jealous.

Jesus followed his father and the good saint into a back room. The counter was filled with various foods from around the globe, but the box of Twinkies sat empty. Jesus said, "Shoot," and tossed the empty box into a trash can under the sink. He pulled an orange from a bowl and began to peel it.

Peter busied himself getting the tea and coffee, carrying the three cups. God took his cup in both hands and felt its warmth. "Thanks."

"She's going to sit there awhile," Peter said.

"Probably," God said, sipping from his cup. He added some sugar from the bowl in the center of the table.

Jesus saw his father scowling. "It's hard for some people."

Peter asked, "Did you invent anger or did that just come with the package?"

"I gave them a world and everything in it," God said. "Everything after that was a choice."

"Still not sure I get that," Peter said.

God looked at him. "Give me your mug for a second."

Peter handed it over carefully, so as not to spill on the hands that created all things. God spun it around in his hands. It was a large blue mug with the words *St. Pete Has Been Good To Me* in large friendly letters. Beneath those it said *St. Petersburg, Florida*.

"You know where this came from," God said. It wasn't a question.

Peter nodded. "You gave it to me...after your vacation a few years back."

"That's right," God said. "Every time I come in here I see you with this cup. That makes me happy to know you enjoy it so much. A few years ago I noticed a crack in the handle." He traced it with his finger. "It looks like you dropped it at some point."

Pete nodded. "When Hitchens came up."

Jesus smirked. "I remember that. Dude was sweatin' bullets."

"But you glued it back in place and you still use it all the time.

That makes me even more happy to know that you appreciated the gift so much you chose to put it back together after you broke it."

Jesus said nothing. He knew where this was going. He sipped his coffee quietly and thought about other broken mugs.

God said, "I give people so many gifts. They don't appreciate them. They don't use them. And if they dropped one and it broke they would just sweep it up and throw it away. People just can't do that to each other."

"So tell them."

"He did," Jesus and God said at the same time while pointing at each other. They looked at each other and smiled. "You owe me a coke. No, you do." They said it in tandem.

"But to teach them when they get up here...isn't that a lesson learned too late?"

"Yeah," God said. He handed the cup back to Peter, who didn't notice that the broken handle was now whole again. "How is Abigail doing?"

"Speaking of broken mugs?" Peter asked. God looked at him over his own teacup and Peter's smile faded. "She's jittery."

"Probably will be," Jesus said. He was wondering if there might be Twinkies in one of the cupboards.

"She works well," Peter said. "I'm not saying she doesn't. I mean she still hasn't gotten used to the idea that she's here yet."

"She's sitting on a lot of questions," Jesus offered.

God leaned back in his chair and slipped his hands into the pockets of his cargo shorts. He sighed. Mary Magdalene usually called this his "pondering face."

God stared at his coffee and then his eyes brightened. He looked over at his son with a "Hey!" expression.

"What?" Jesus asked.

The Father of all Creation said, "I just had an idea."

Chapter

(3)

...a little bit later on.

Jesus walked into God's workshop. He didn't knock. If his father was busy or did not want to be disturbed there would be no door to knock on. At the moment there was a door and it stood wide open, which was just as well because it had no doorknob. Also, the creator liked company when he was creating.

God sat at his potter's wheel. It spun around to the faint hum of an electric motor. God wore a heavy apron looped over his neck and draped over his legs. It was covered in smears of dried clay, but the words on the front were clearly readable. They said *Kiss the Cook*. His hair was pulled back into a ponytail and tied with a bright sparkly elastic band. (A little girl named Carol had taken it off her own hair and dropped it into the offering plate one Sunday morning.) Some of his long hair had fallen in his face. There was a smudge of clay on his forehead where God had tried to tuck the strand behind his ear.

Wet clay clumped around the edges of his fingernails and flecks of gray were scattered up his arms. Jesus stood and silently watched his father work. The glob of clay slowly grew and became a sort of bowl. Then the master's hands brought the edges together and carefully raised the object up to become a vase.

Music came from a small black radio on the nearby tabletop. "You know," Jesus said, "that you have a multitude of musicians who could come in here and play you any song you want."

"I like Public Radio," God said. "The classics are the best. Nobody writes symphonies for my glory anymore."

"Feeling a bit full of ourselves, aren't we?" Jesus said.

"I'll take Mozart," God said. "All the hip-hop artists thank *you* anyway."

"I'll take The Who," Jesus said. "Speaking of...where is Keith Moon?"

God said, "He and Ludwig are on tour."

"In heaven?" Jesus asked, sounding surprised.

"Dreams," God said. "Lud likes to play in kids' dreams. Takes a rocker along for a beat."

"Nice job with that whole music thing," Jesus said. "One of your better ideas, really."

"I am the Father of all Creation," God said.

At that moment the vase he was working on became unstable and fell in upon itself. God looked at the mess and switched the motor off with a clay-encrusted finger. He sighed and looked at the mess in front of him. "Shoot," God said. The Lord scooped the clay off the wheel and began to press the scraps back together. After a moment the broken pot was now a smooth round ball again.

"Yeah, but do people ask WWGD?"

"I suppose not," God said. "Sounds awfully close to taking my name in vain. Are people still doing the WWJD thing?"

"Some," Jesus said. "The kids that started it are. Most people quit wearing the necklaces. Now it's kind of a joke."

"WWJD for a Klondike bar?"

"Heard that one."

God leaned back in his chair. "Ahhhhhhh....Who Would Jesus Date?"

"Where Would Jesus Dine?" the son said and started to smile. The game was on.

"Wet and Wild Jelly Donuts," God said.

"When Will Jupiter Drop?" Jesus replied.

"What's With Jesus, Diarrhea?" God said.

"Eww!" Jesus said.

"It fits," God told him. "Your turn."

"Ahhhh...."

"Come on! Come on!" the Creator taunted.

Jesus said, "Willy Wonka Just Died."

"Shoot!" God said. He touched his forehead to think and left a clay blotch there. "Ummmmmmmm…."

"Five seconds," Jesus said.

"We never set a time limit."

"Beeeeeeeeeeep," Jesus buzzed. "I win."

"We never set a time limit," God said.

Jesus said, "What? I'm going to give you all day?

"I'm an old man," God said. "I need extra time."

Jesus smiled at his father, "You're as young as you feel."

"I'm feeling old these days," God said. Jesus let the silence hang for a moment and then walked over to a small dorm room refrigerator. He opened it and removed a bottle of ice tea.

"You want something?" Jesus asked

"Is there one of those Starbucks coffee thingies in there?"

"Last one." Jesus held it up.

"That's fine."

The son of the Creator of the Universe shook the small can of coffee for his father. He reached into a cupboard above the refrigerator and found a package of plastic straws. Opening the can, he put the straw in and held it up for his Father to sip from so the creator did not need to take his hands from the clay again.

"Ahhhhhhhhhh," said God. "Thanks!"

"Don't mention it," Jesus said, and set the can on the counter next to the Lord.

"She here yet?" Jesus asked.

"Not yet," God said.

"You got mud on you when you tapped your forehead," Jesus said.

God reached up and wiped his forehead with the back of his wrist and looked at it. "Hazard of the trade."

"There's nobody else in your trade," Jesus offered.

"Glorified camp counselor?" God asked.

"Creator of the Universe."

"Feels more like being a waiter some days."

Jesus said, "You made the days."

"Long time ago," his father said. God rolled the clay ball up onto the end of his finger, where it stopped and hovered impossibly. God took his hand away and allowed the ball to float. For a moment Jesus thought he might create a world but he caught it again and absentmindedly tossed it back and forth in his hands.

"You made all of creation in just six days," Jesus said, leaning against the sink.

God shrugged. "Could have done it in four, but I slept in a few times."

Jesus was smiling. He liked teasing his father this way. "You made the sun so it could come up in the morning and you could keep track of the days."

God, who had learned to ignore his son when he got like this, said, "I made the sun because I don't like to work in the dark. And it's not fun to sleep in if it's going to be dark when you get up."

Jesus said, "And the moon?"

"I wanted to make something for the romantics."

"There were no romantics when you made the moon."

God said, "Pre-planning."

Jesus finished his drink and tossed it in the air toward the green recycling bin. The shot was wide of the mark and the bottle turned in midair and set itself gently down on top of the other glass bottles. "Well, I'm outta here."

God looked up. "You have someplace to go?"

Jesus said, "John Lennon is giving a concert."

God shook his head. "Abigail is going to be here in a minute."

Jesus said, "You sure you want to do this? You haven't gotten this personally involved with the angels in a while."

"Abigail is special," God said. "She seems disappointed. Nobody is supposed to be disappointed when they get up here."

"Your Majesty?"

Both God and the Savior turned to see a red-headed angel standing at the door of the workshop. She was dressed in a floor-length but shapeless white gown that seem to blaze in its complete and total whiteness. She had wings made of fluffy white feathers that arched above her head and flowed down to the hem of her robe in the back. Her halo seemed to be made of Christmas tinsel, like the haloes in Sunday School Christmas pageants. She held a clipboard.

"Did you hear that?" God asked. "She said 'Your Majesty'. Now that's what I call respect for your elders."

Jesus rolled his eyes. "I have to go. There's an angel here to see you."

God set the glob of clay down on the wheel. "You'd pass up quality time with your father to go to some rock concert with your friends?" He looked at Abigail and shook his head. "Kids these days."

Abigail looked everywhere in the room except at the Father and the Son. "St. Peter asked me to get your signature on a few things."

God smiled. "Did he now?"

Abigail stared at a spot of wet clay on the floor. "Yes, Your Majesty."

God said, "It's all right, my dear. You can look at me."

She did. She saw his face and she smiled.

God looked her over. "Well, don't you have your grandmother's smile?

Abigail asked, "You know my grandmother?"

God said, "My dear, I know everyone. You are Abigail."

Abigail nodded.

"Do you prefer Abby or Abigail?

"Either one is fine."

God wiped his hands on the leather apron. He reached out and took the clipboard from Abigail. She saw the fingerprints he was leaving on the clipboard and smiled. That was going to make Peter nuts.

Jesus looked from his father to Abigail. "You're new. I saw you at the Welcome Station."

Abigail looked at the Amy Grant T-shirt that Jesus was wearing. "Yes, sir."

Jesus to God, "She called me *sir!*"

God did not look up from the forms. "She doesn't know you yet."

Jesus turned back to Abigail. "Do you like Heaven so far?"

Abigail seemed to smile a little. "It's so big."

"You ain't seen nothing yet," Jesus and God said at the same time. God said, "Jinx! You owe me a coke."

Abigail said, "I can't wait to go exploring."

Jesus nodded. "There's stuff I haven't seen yet, and I've been here for a while now. It changes all the time."

God said, "You're welcome" without looking up.

Abigail looked from Jesus to God.

Jesus said, "He creates an ever-expanding universe and then thinks he can take credit for everything."

"You're welcome," God repeated.

Jesus leaned over and opened the refrigerator again. "Do you like working at the Welcome Station?"

"That better not be my last Sweet Tea," God said, flipping the page.

"You can get more."

"They don't make Milo's Sweet Tea in cans."

Jesus waited. God looked up and wondered why his son was staring at him.

"Oh, yeah," God said. "Go ahead. Abigail, would you like something to drink?"

"No thank you," Abigail said.

Jesus leaned on the sink again. "Sorry, I think I interrupted you. Do you like working at the Welcome Station?"

"It looks like the Welcome Station in Jacksonville, Florida."

"That's what I told him."

God was still looking at the forms and making notes in the margins. "Our orange juice is better."

"And there are more brochures."

God looked up from his forms at Jesus, who looked back at him. "She's quick. I like her."

Abigail said, "I never thought it would really have pearly gates."

"They aren't really pearly gates. It just gives people something to talk about when they're in line."

Abigail said, "And I never thought there'd be a line. St. Peter sits there with this really big book and he looks up their name in the book."

God looked up. "Actually he doesn't even need to do that. But we found some folks really like to see Peter look their names up in a big book."

Abigail looked at the floor again. "And the button that says *Trap Door to Hell?*"

God chuckled. "That was funny."

Jesus said, "Well, I'm off to see Mr. Lennon."

"Tell him that we really do exist up here," God said.

Jesus looked at Abigail. "He never gets tired of that joke."

Abigail tilted her head. "Imagine that."

Jesus and God traded looks. God said, "I do like her."

Jesus smiled and went through the workshop door.

"Now, my dear, would you happen to have a red pen with you? I think I need to underline a few things."

"New commandments?" Abigail asked?

"Same old same old," God said.

Abigail lifted her white robe and dug a pen out of her jeans pocket.

God seemed surprised. "You're wearing jeans?"

Abigail looked like she'd been caught passing a note in class. "Is that okay?"

God said, "This is heaven, my dear, of course it's okay. I was going to ask you about the wings."

Abigail said, "I feel like a Q-tip."

God said, "Gabriel goes for the big wings. Did he suggest you wear those?"

"Yes, Your Majesty."

God smiled. "You don't have to call me Your Majesty."

"What should I call you?"

God said, "I have many names."

Abigail looked at the ceiling and counted on her fingers. "Jehovah, Elohim, The great *I Am*...."

God said, "Hmmmmmm. Sounds like somebody went to Sunday school."

Abigail said, "What name do you like?"

God thought for a moment. No one asked *him* that. "I sort of like Abba."

Abigail said, "That means father."

"Actually, it's closer to the word 'Daddy', but you're right."

"I'll call you Abba," Abigail announced.

God said, "Wonderful. You know, sweetheart, you don't have to wear the robe and wings if you don't want to. It's not a uniform."

Abigail looked down. "I thought this is what angels wear."

God smiled. "We really are pretty informal around here."

Abigail said, "I was expecting streets of gold." There was a window to her left and Abigail went and stood beside it. A field of stars seemed to shimmer at her.

God said, "Public relations. Didn't expect people to take it so seriously." God gathered the clay from the wheel in front of him and began to work it back and forth in his hands.

Without looking away from the stars beyond the window, Abigail said, "I'm sure my grandma was disappointed."

"She got over it."

"Can I see her?"

God nodded. "Eventually."

Abigail turned and smiled at him. "Can I have a car?"

"Eventually."

Abigail leaned in a dramatic pose against the windowsill and lifted her bare foot into the air. "Can I have a house on the beach with cabana boys rubbing my feet and feeding me grapes?"

God looked at her and shrugged. "Eventually."

Abigail stood. "When is eventually?"

God said, "When you are ready."

She looked down and grabbed a handful of white robe. "Can I lose this thing?"

God chuckled. "Of course. This is heaven."

Abigail reached up and pulled the wings over her head. They got tangled in the robe for a moment and she began to try to punch her way out. She finally freed herself and brushed her long hair back away from her face as if to say, "I meant to do that." She laid the wings and the robe over a chair near the table.

God studied her. "Don't forget the halo."

Abigail said, "I like the halo."

God continued to play with the ball of clay. "Okay then. Would you like something to eat?"

"No thank you, Abba."

God said, "Are you sure? You can have anything you want. Pizza, double chocolate chip cookies, ice cream."

"I don't like ice cream."

"You don't have to have any. This is heaven. Would you like to sit down? I like to have someone to talk to when I'm in my workshop."

Abigail looked uncomfortable. "Uh… I think I'm supposed to go back to work. The forms, you know?"

God said, "You really don't need the job. Once you get acclimated you can explore the universe."

Abigail looked out the window again. "What about all the angels working at the Welcome Station?"

"Former DMV workers…every one of them."

Abigail laughed. "You're kidding."

"Yes."

Abigail looked at him, waiting for more.

God hooked his clay-covered thumbs in the straps of his leather apron. "You see, my dear, some people are only happy when they are working. If they want a job they can have a job. If they want to surf the stars and watch the sunrise from the moon they can do that. Sometimes we give new arrivals jobs until they get their feet under them, so to speak."

Abigail asked, "When can I explore?"

God said, "When you're ready.

"When am I ready?"

God smiled. "Have a cold drink. Sit down. Come and let us reason together."

"Huh?"

God said, "Let's talk."

Abigail hesitated for a moment, then said, "What have you got to drink?"

"This is heaven, my dear. Whatever you want is in there."

Abigail asked, "Strawberry Yoo Hoo?"

"One left."

"There was only one left the last time you offered me one."

"It's a refrigerator in heaven, dear," God said. "There's always one more."

Abigail walked over to the refrigerator and opened it. There in front of all the coffees, teas, and Snapples was a frosty Strawberry Yoo-Hoo. Abigail took it and then asked "Hey, what's a Pepsi AM?"

"Extra caffeine," God said. "They test marketed it once but never made it a regular thing. I liked it. I work best in the mornings."

Abigail floated over and sat in the chair quietly. God rolled the clay back and forth in his hands. Finally the silence got to her. "This is weird," she said.

"What is?"

"I thought I had so many questions."

God smiled.

"What are you making?" Abigail asked.

"It's called *Roy's Life.*"

"You mean that literally."

"Yes," God said. "This is Roy's life." God then took the ball of clay and slammed it down hard onto the surface of the potter's wheel.

Abigail winced. "That was a little cruel, wasn't it?"

God ignored her. "He's going through a rough time," God said, prying the flattened clay from the wheel.

He slammed the clay a second time. "His car repair bill is higher than his paycheck."

Slam.

"He and his wife fight a lot."

Slam.

"He lost a big account at work."

Slam.

"He lost his job."

Slam.

"His wife left him."

Abigail said, "You have a tendency to pick on certain people. You know that?"

"Only those who can take it," God said. He had molded the clay into a ball once again. A thin wire was stretched between two points on the wheel housing. God took the clay ball and sliced it in two with the wire. He looked at the two halves. There in the center was a tiny space.

"A-ha!" God said, and pointed the space out to the young angel.

"What's *a-ha*?"

"See that little air pocket? It's good I caught that now. Roy has something deeper that needs fixing. If I hadn't caught that, Roy would have exploded in the furnace. He would have taken out several others with him." God mashed the halves back together. He rolled them into a ball and forcefully put the ball back on the wheel with one last...slam.

"Is that it?" Abigail asked.

"That's it," God said. He flipped the switch with his knee and the wheel began to spin.

God wet his hands in the water and slowly and gently touched the spinning mound of clay. "Finally he's ready to listen to me."

"So when he finally comes to you with nothing left..."

"That's when we can start to work."

The Lord's massive hands held the mound in place and then he slowly started to bring them together. "He's going to go back to school," God said.

The mound got higher. God pressed his fingers into the top of the spinning clay and began to hollow it out.

"He's getting inside himself. He's getting some counseling."

Abigail nodded, fascinated by the way her "Abba" worked.

As the mound of clay became a jar, a small piece of clay came loose and curled around the top of the opening.

"Get that," Abigail said. She was caught up in Roy's life.

"It's okay," God said. "He's strong. He can handle it. It's nothing."

The Creator reached over and picked up a small metal tool with a wire no thicker than a paper clip. He cautiously touched the end of the wire to the top of the vase and the loose piece trimmed off and fell to the spinning wheel where it rolled out of the way.

"What was that?" Abigail asked.

"A little pain. A little anger. He's done with them. He's held onto them for a long time but he doesn't need them any more anyway."

The potter's hands carefully embraced the jar and lightly squeezed it together. The neck of the vase grew in the Master's hands.

"This is where he lost it before," Abigail said.

"I know," God said. "But we're working together this time."

God's hands brought the neck of the vase up slowly. Not too far. Not too fast. Not beyond its own ability to hold itself. God pulled his hands away and picked up a sponge. He touched it lightly to the vase and the blemishes and lines disappeared. The clay became smooth as glass. God flicked the switch and the table stopped.

"Now what?" Abigail asked.

"We give Roy some time," God said. "We let him dry and get a little more sturdy. Then he goes into the fire. Which will hurt. But he's strong and clean. He knows it's temporary. He knows what's ahead for him."

"And then?"

"Then he'll hold flowers or treasure or whatever he wants to hold," God said proudly.

"Is there one of me?" Abigail asked.

"There was," God said. There was very little emotion in his voice. Neither disappointment nor anger. He was simply stating a fact.

"And what happens to the vase?"

God shrugged. "I'll give it to him as a housewarming gift when he gets up here. It'll look nice on his table with some roses. Don't you think?"

Abigail said nothing. She sipped her Yoo Hoo. God went over to the sink and began to wash his hands. He cleaned the clay from beneath his fingernails and studied the shelves of jars and vases that lined the wall. He smiled to himself and continued to scrub.

When Saint Peter floated into the room without knocking it startled Abigail so much that she nearly dropped her bottle. Peter's robe was perfect. His wings were perfect. His long platinum blonde hair was perfect. There wasn't a wrinkle on him anywhere. The only part of him that didn't look outright beautiful was the look on his face. The only word Abigail could think of to describe it was "peeved." He had a pencil behind his ear and was carrying another clipboard of forms.

"There you are. I sent you to get a signature, not to bother the Creator of the Universe."

God was still washing his hands in the deep sink. "She's not bothering me, Peter."

St. Peter said, "Did you give him the forms?"

Abigail started, "I..."

St. Peter said, "Oh don't give me that....Where are your wings!"

Abigail tried again. "I..."

St. Peter said, "People like the wings. People want to see the wings. They like the big book of names and they like the wings. People who come up have certain expectations, young lady; it is our job to make them feel welcome and comfortable."

Abigail said, "I don't do expectations."

Peter glared at her.

"I have the halo," Abigail said meekly. She smiled and pointed to the bobbing decoration on top of her head.

St. Peter said, "You can't wear the halo without the wings. That's not even a proper halo. You need to go see Michael about a proper halo. That's Christmas tinsel. What's holding it on your head?"

"Pipe cleaners."

"*Pipe cleaners?* You're in heaven. You can have the light of the stars encircling your head. You can have..."

God interrupted. "I like the halo on her. It's cute." He was drying his hands now and checking to see if there was still clay under his fingernails. Abigail thought he spotted some, but then he chose to leave it there.

"People like wings. People like halos," Peter said again.

God said, "People need to get an after-life."

Abigail laughed into her hand.

Peter, the one to whom Jesus had said, "On you I'll build my church," said to the creator, "It doesn't do anything for my authority when you make jokes in front of the help."

God looked annoyed at his son's best friend. "She's not the help. She's an angel and I asked her to keep me company."

Peter said, "How will we get anything done if you keep giving my angels coffee breaks?"

God said, "I think you can get by."

St. Peter looked over at Abigail and then back to God. "You'll send my new angel back when you are done, right?"

God smiled. "Of course."

Peter reached up and straightened his own halo, which he had dimmed when he came into the workshop. Normally he kept it so bright that people who came up to the big book had to shield their eyes. Peter would then sit up straighter and dim the halo. This would make people look at his face. At this point he would look at them in joy or with his best "You-are-so-totally-screwed" face, depending on his mood. He floated out of the room shaking his head.

God looked apologetically at Abigail. "He has a lot of stress."

Abigail was still looking at the door to see if Peter "brightened" as he went around the corner. He did. She turned back to God. "But this is heaven."

God said, "Different things make us happy." He paused and said, "May I ask you a question?"

"Sure," she said.

"When Peter mentioned about people having expectations, you said 'I don't do expectations'. What does that mean?"

Abigail looked off out the window again. "I never felt like I lived up to them."

God asked, "Whose?"

"Anybody's. My mom's. My dad's. Society's."

God nodded and sat down in front of the angel. She felt very small next to him. "And their expectations mattered because…"

Abigail felt defensive. "You have to be a certain thing to get ahead in the world."

God said, "Why?"

"Because you do. You have to study to get the grades on the standardized tests, so you can get into the good college, so you can get the good job."

"And whose expectations are those?"

"My mother's. Society's."

God said, "I see. Any other expectations?"

Abigail looked unsure. "Yeah...well...yours."

God looked surprised. "Mine?"

"Yeah."

"What did I want from you?" God asked.

Abigail suddenly felt as if she might cry, but she buried it down. "We're supposed to be perfect and goody-goody all the time."

"Were you perfect?"

"No."

"Are you here?"

"Yes," she said. The word came out a little more "spoiled" than she wanted it to.

God looked at her. "And the definition of grace is...?"

Abigail said nothing.

God stood up and went to the window. "People make a whole lot of rules in my name, Abigail. I don't ask them for a lot. I want my children to look out for each other, I want them to be the best they can be, and a 'thank you' once in a while wouldn't hurt. That's what I expect. If people can't handle that, I forgive them."

Abigail stood up to go.

"Abigail."

The angel turned and looked at him.

"Answer me honestly. Do you like working in the Welcome Station?"

"Not so much," she said quietly.

"I've got some errands to run dirt-side," he said. "Would you like to come along?"

She hesitated.

"I've got a car," God said. Abigail's tinsel halo began to shimmer.

Chapter

God stood at the far edge of heaven. Well, as much as there can be an "edge" to something that's limitless. God and Abigail stood there together. Watching the prayers come up. The edge was constantly alive with activity. To a casual observer it looked like chaos, but if you simply stood and watched for a while you would see the order in the chaos. Saints and angels crowded around the opening as the prayers came up. Some prayers seemed to have great difficulty, as if they weighed more than the others. The struggle inside was evident. Some shot up like T-shirts being fired at a semi-pro baseball game crowd. Some were immediately answered. Some were not. Some were carefully filed away. Some seemed to almost get away until angels with multiple sets of wings flew after them, retrieved them, cradled them like lost children and brought them back.

New arrivals loved to watch the prayers. It was one of the first stops on the tour when they arrived. For many, most in fact, it was the most beautiful thing they had ever seen. Most then promptly forgot about the prayer stop when they reached "heaven proper." Some returned. Usually to hear from relatives. Sometimes just to watch.

God stood on the edge of heaven in his favorite hooded pullover. It was woven from a beach blanket or some other material. It was soft and had a pocket on the front. The hood was large and the creator could pull it down over his eyes and look like a monk... well, if a monk wore a blue stripe robe.

His feet were bare and he curled his toes over the edge and allowed the prayers to wash over him. Not exactly listening, but feeling them like a breeze as they blew through his long white hair.

Abigail stood a little ways back behind God. She was overcome in her amazement of the vision before her. She did not remember seeing the prayers when she arrived. She didn't remember getting a tour.

Without opening his eyes God said, "It's okay, Abigail. I know you're there."

"I didn't want to disturb you."

"You're not." God turned around. "And you've chosen to keep the wings I see."

"Smaller," Abigail said. "The big ones looked like a yogurt commercial."

"And the tattoo? You kept the tattoo but lost the nose ring."

"I like the tattoo," the young angel said. "The nose ring was just to make my mom mad."

"Jeans and a T-shirt," God said. "Nice look. Jesus will appreciate it."

"Is he going to be here?" Abby asked.

"Later," God said. "For now it's you and me. Do you remember this place?"

Abigail looked at Heaven's Edge as if she hadn't seen it when she came in.

"It's beautiful. I've never seen anything like it."

"It's on the tour," God said.

"I don't remember much about the tour. Some of it's still a blur. I don't even remember going through the Welcome Station."

God nodded. "You came up another way. Some do that."

"What do you mean, 'another way'?" Abby asked.

"Come here."

Abigail floated down next to the creator on her tiny wings and stood with the tips of her converse high-tops poking over the edge. She had a strong desire to reach out and hold God's hand as if she were about to cross a busy street for the first time, but she pushed the urge away.

"Do you know what these are?" God asked.

Abigail shook her head.

God reached out and gently took one of the prayers as it floated up. He held it as gingerly as he would try to hold a soap bubble between his fingers. He carefully pulled it out of the stream and held it near Abby's face. He released it and poked it with is finger. A woman's voice said,

"Please God, let me get this promotion. I really need it this time. I know I asked before, but I really need it. The extra money will be so much of a help to my family."

"It's a prayer?" Abby said in amazement.

God nodded.

Abby looked at the fountain of prayers coming up in front of her. "These are all prayers?"

God nodded again.

"You're losing some," Abby said. She stood and watched as prayers swirled above her head and out of sight. She turned to the creator. There was just a trace of panic in her voice. "I said you're losing some!"

"They're never lost," God said.

Abigail stood there watching the prayers float. She could feel her mind reeling.

"You have a question," God said.

Abigail said, "There are a whole lot of unhappy people in the world, you know?"

God nodded quietly. "Yes, I hear them all the time."

Abigail turned to look up at him. "Why do you permit the suffering?"

God almost smiled. But not really. "I don't permit it, Abigail. You do. I put you all together on one planet. You can love each other or you can kill each other."

"And you just watch from up here?"

"Mostly."

Abigail said, "Then you don't care." She sounded hurt.

God was surprised. "I do care."

Abigail turned away. "How are we supposed to know that?"

"When Jesus gets here he'll show you his scars," God said impatiently.

Abigail crossed her arms. She was trying to think things through that she hadn't before. God could see the spark when she thought of her next question. "Why don't you just make people happy? Don't you think they'd be better followers if they were happy?"

"Boooooooooooooooring."

Abigail pressed it. "People question your existence when bad stuff happens. If you didn't bash them they might believe more."

"I don't make bad stuff happen, Abigail. Bad stuff happens. That's why I gave you each other. If everyone got what they wanted all the time you'd get bored."

Abigail said, "Boring doesn't hurt,"

God reached into the prayer stream and pulled another one out.

A little more forcefully this time. It broke before he could get it to Abigail.

"Don't let them give me a mini-van, God. Let it be a sports car this time. I hate rental cars. Please make them give me something decent this time. Come on God! Something hot."

"What am I—a waiter?" God said. "Please please *please* give me this or give me that." God pulled out another one. Gently this time.

"My husband is a good man, Lord. I love him so much. Please don't take him. I don't know what I'll do without him, God. Please. Please, God."

Abigail looked at the prayer as it swirled in the Father's hand. Then she looked up at his face. She couldn't read the expression. Was it pity? Sadness? Disappointment? God gently tossed the prayer into the air. It floated up with the others.

"Do they think I'm not here? Do they think I don't know what I'm doing? Whatever happened to 'thy will be done'? They say it every Sunday but they don't want it to be true if it's gonna hurt. There are farmers who pray every Sunday for rain but they don't take an umbrella to church. What happened to faith?"

"It's not about faith," Abigail said. "It's about proof. Why can't you just give us a full-out definite *I'm here* moment?"

"I did," God said. "You crucified him."

"So now I get blame for what people did like a thousand years ago?"

"Faith is believing without proof," God said.

"It doesn't always work that way," Abigail said. She looked at him with an "is-this-our-first-fight" kind of look. Suddenly a prayer came up from below that was different than the others. Abby could see it was a different color. Meaning it was a color she had never seen before. God reached into the stream with both hands and gently scooped it out. He held it softly as if it were a broken bird. Bringing it between them, he gently opened it.

"God, what is wrong with me? Why is my father doing this? Please take me away. Please God. Let me live with my Aunt Violet or let me and Mom just go away. Please God. I don't want to live here anymore. Not with him. Please make him stop."

The prayer swirled around and then dissolved in God's palm.

"Answered?" Abigail asked.

"No," God said. "I gave her some peace. She's got important things to do someday and she's got to go through some bad stuff to get there."

"Is this a vase thing?"

God nodded and smiled at her like an algebra teacher whose student had just solved the simplest equation. "Yes," he said. "A vase thing."

Abigail was quiet for a long time. Then she finally said, "So, what do you want to do? People have forgotten what prayer is about. They don't say 'thanks' or 'nice to know ya' or 'I am your servant' but they're not all selfish, are they?"

"No," said God. "And some do remember to say 'thank you.' Some even say 'I am your servant' and mean it."

"So?" Abigail said. "What do you do?"

God took his hands out of his shirt pouch and rubbed them through his long white hair. Whether it was in frustration or habit Abigail did not know.

"Sometimes I give them what they want. Sometimes I give them what they need. And sometimes I give them what I give them."

"What is it *you* want?" God looked at her. He hadn't had anyone ask him that earnestly in a long time. He had heard "what is it you want from *me*?" and he had heard the question as if the person was bargaining, but no one had simply asked him what *he* wanted in a long time.

"I want to be believed in," God said. "They do a survey that says 98% of the world believes in me, but basically, they're just practical atheists. They don't believe that I actually have an effect on their everyday lives."

"But you let them make the choices," Abigail said. "If you let things go the way they go, why should they think you are there all the time?"

"*I* let things go," God said. "*I* do. *I* let them make decisions. *I* let them live with the consequences. Do they think any of that would be possible if I didn't put it all in place?"

"They don't think about that at all," Abigail said. "They don't choose to ignore you. They just don't think about it. You want them to put it in your hands, but you want them to use the hands that you gave them too. It can get confusing."

"I want them to know that life is a gift. I won't make a decision for their lives without consulting them first. I want them to cherish each other. I want them to improve themselves. I want them to make their own decisions, but only if they will help each other. I want them to love each other and stop fighting."

"You sound like a parent."

"Go figure," God said.

"You're not always easy to love," Abigail said. "People are selfish."

"Some are," God said. "Some are my servants and go where I send them and do what they are told. Others just don't understand why it has to hurt sometimes and would rather sit at home and lick their wounds."

The two of them stood and watched the prayers come up for a little while longer. God turned to leave. "Okay," he said. "That's the lesson for today."

Abigail stood there and watched him walk away. "What do you mean that's it for today?" she said to his back. "It was just getting interesting."

"Tomorrow," God said. "We go have French toast. Be ready. We leave before sunrise."

"I thought you made the sun rise," she said, but by that time he was somewhere else.

The prayers swirled up into the stars on their own. Soon the angels and the saints returned with the lost ones. Some were scooped up from the floor, barely able to make the journey.

And all things continued to go on as they always do.

Chapter

Abigail stood next to the Creator of All Things. The great *I Am*. The *Is*. The Father Almighty. She was pretty sure she had a booger the size of Pittsburgh in her nose but was too embarrassed to get it out. God had his hands in the pockets of his khaki shorts. His feet were bare, as were hers. They stood at the edge where the beach ends and the water begins. She imagined it could probably work the other way around, too. They were at the spot where the beach begins and the water ends. It could work that way. Depending on which way you were facing. She wondered if it was a half-empty half-full lesson. She wondered if the giant booger was hanging out of her nostril. She wondered if anyone could see them.

She began to fidget like a child in church. Shifting from one foot to the other. God simply stood. He said nothing. She didn't know why she had been invited along. God, or Abba as she called him, said something about French Toast, but she wasn't sure there was a lesson to be learned. She had not been allowed to wear the wings...or the halo. She liked the wings, and imagined since they were heading to earth she might be able to show them off. Perhaps a quick zip over to her Sunday School teacher's (Mrs. Coldiron) house to just say "See! I am *so* in."

The waves came up and wet the end of the Creator's toes. She didn't know why they were here but she did know it was too damn early. The sun had come almost all the way up, but it was still a bright orange ball you could stare at without burning out your retinas.

Their shoes were twenty feet behind them sitting under two beach chairs. God's eyes were closed. The wind from the waves blew his long white hair in his face but he didn't seem to mind. She began to fidget again, wondering what she was supposed to say or do. Or did he want her to say something or ask a question?

"Just relax," he said, as if he was reading her discomfort. He didn't just say "just relax." It came out as sort of a "juuuuust relaaaaaaaaax." His voice was really deep. He sounded like one of the Wayne Dyer CDs her mother used to listen to. Abigail would watch her mother sit there with her head back and say "Ahhhhhhhhhhhhhhhhhhhhhhhhhhhhh" and she would giggle and then her mother would get mad and make her go to her room.

Abigail tried. She took a deep breath. She liked the smell of the water but it seemed to stoke her already impatient attitude.

"You know," he said slowly and deeply, "I love the beach. I loved it when I made it. I spent the Sabbath here."

"Which Sabbath?" She asked.

"The first one," he said. "As in 'on the seventh day I rested.' It was on the beach. I think what I like most about it is that you can stand here and it looks pretty much the same as the day I made it."

Abigail looked out into the ocean and tried to imagine what it was like the first time the water rolled in. God opened his eyes. "I know if I turn around I'll see that me-awful hotel and the city beyond it, but if you just stand right here and look out that way..." He breathed in deeply and blew it out slowly. "It hasn't changed all that much."

He breathed deep again. This time Abigail did too.

"I said it before and I'll say it again," God said. "This is good."

Behind them someone said, "Beautiful isn't it?" Both Abby and God turned and saw an older man standing about ten feet back. "Didn't mean to bother," he said. The old man had a jacket on that seemed like it may have fit him in his younger days but was now too big. He leaned on a cane on which he had nailed a flat piece of wood to give him balance on the sand.

"It's lovely," God said.

"I never get tired of watching that sun come up," the old man said. "I come here every day."

"You're a lucky man," God said.

"When you get to be my age you learn to appreciate the little things."

"Little?" God said. "Can you imagine the work that went into a plan like this?" Abigail was appreciating the irony. God winked at her. He said it as if he was making a joke. "The complete order of the universe laid out so that a great ball of mud and water loops around a great ball of burning gas, turning one revolution in exactly twenty-four hours. And then to realize that's only the tip of the iceberg. I hardly think it's a little thing."

The old man looked at God and then back at the sunrise. The Creator had been trying to make a joke but the old man took it very seriously. "You're right. Sometimes I forget how big God is."

Abigail smiled.

"I don't think I've seen you two here. Maybe I just don't remember," the old man said.

"Oh, I haven't been here in years," God said. "My son comes here quite a bit. We thought we would meet him today and see if he wants to get some breakfast."

"Place up the road," the old man said, "has the best French Toast you've ever had."

"Lorena's Diner?" God asked.

The old man nodded. "That's the place. Imported maple syrup."

"I know Lorena's well," God said. "But it's been years, like I said. My son goes there quite a bit."

"Young fella? About thirty? Has a beard like yours?" the old man asked.

"That would be him." God said.

"I see him a lot," the old man said. "You've got a nice boy there."

"Thanks," said God.

"I'm Daniel," the old man said. He held out his hand to God.

"Avery," God said. "Avery Mann." They shook hands.

"This my student, Abigail," God said.

"Abigail," the old man repeated. "My wife had hair about your color. It's very pretty."

"Thank you," Abigail said cordially.

"Student, huh?" Daniel asked. "Let me guess. Art?"

"Art. Cooking. And some philosophy," Abigail said.

"You retired?" Daniel asked God.

"Well, nobody ever really retires. Do they, Daniel?"

Daniel laughed. "No, I guess they don't. I was in the retail business. Every now and then I get a great idea and then remember that I'm not going to work so I just let it go."

"Write them down," God said. "Pass them on to someone who can use them."

"They're old ideas from an old man," Daniel said.

"You are just a child," God said. Daniel would have laughed, but he saw how serious his companion was and kept silent. Abigail looked up at God and wondered what it was like to be that old. She wondered what it would have been like to be as old as Daniel.

"Your boy is here," Daniel said.

God and Abigail turned and saw Jesus walking toward them. He wore the same shorts as God did. A Hawaiian shirt hung open in front of another one of his Amy Grant concert T-shirts. He had tied the strings of his shoes together and hung them around his neck. His hands were in his pockets. He walked so the surf came up to his ankles. He smiled when he saw the trio waiting for him.

"He favors you," Daniel said.

"A lot of people say that," God said.

"Hey, Pop!" Jesus said. The son of the Creator of the Universe enveloped his Father in a warm embrace. He turned to Abigail and offered a more polite but still loving hug. "Abby. Good to see you again."

Abigail stood there for a moment, still feeling the hug even after he had let go of her. Somewhere deep in her brain something said, "You know that guy you used to sing songs about in Vacation Bible School? That guy who, last year, you said never existed? Do you remember that guy? You just hugged him."

She felt his warmth even after she had let go. She wondered if this was what people felt after he had touched them in all those Bible stories. She wondered if he knew he had that effect. She wondered if he felt it go out of him.

"Daniel, it's good to see you." Jesus reached out his hand and shook with his friend.

"Jesse," Daniel said.

"How's the arthritis?" Jesus asked.

"Good days and bad days," Daniel said. "Thanks for the idea for the cane. It helps a lot. You should patent it or something."

Jesus smiled.

God said, "I thought I'd meet you. See if you want to have breakfast with us."

"After a while," Jesus said. "I need to take a walk."

"Okay," God said. "Our chairs are right up there if you want to leave your shoes."

Jesus looked at the chair in the sand. "If I did that I'd have to take my feet out of the water," he said. He looked to make sure Daniel wasn't looking and then rose up and stood on the water's surface. He grinned and winked at Abigail who looked at God to see if he thought it was funny. "I'll be back in about twenty minutes or so. Good to see you, Daniel."

"You too," Daniel said, and they watched the carpenter move on down the beach. "He's a good boy."

"Yes, he is."

"Can I ask you something, I mean, if you don't think I'm too forward?"

"Go ahead," God said.

"I noticed your son has scars on his wrists. That's how we lost my boy back in '77."

"I'm sorry," God said.

"It's okay," Daniel said. "Your Jesse reminds me a lot of my Zack. Zack never seemed to find religion the way your boy did. I don't mean all that chanting and stuff. My wife would have kicked him out if she heard him speaking Hebrew one day and chanting Catholic the next."

Abigail looked surprised. It never occurred to her that Jesus still prayed. She digested that information and tried to see if it made sense to her. Jesus prayed in the Bible, right? Technically, he was a Christian. She also guessed that he would do a bit of everything. "It makes him feel connected, I guess," God said.

Daniel nodded. "Zack used to pray out there," he said, looking out toward the ocean. "He liked to surf. Said it was the one place he felt close to God."

God suddenly remembered Zack. "Yes," he said, "It's a very good place to pray."

"He got angry at God after his mother died," Daniel said. "After that he just sort of withdrew into himself."

God remembered that too.

"I imagine they know each other again now."

"You think so?" Daniel said. For just a moment Abigail thought there was just a trace of hope in his voice. "My Mrs. always said that suicides don't get in."

Abigail suddenly looked down at the shells in the surf. The warmth of Jesus' hug was fully gone and she felt a wave of emptiness so severe that she thought she might cry.

"People make up a lot of rules in the name of God," the Lord said.

"God's rules were pretty simple...love me and love each other. Then there's that whole grace thing. I've never understood why people like to make big long lists of rules and then act like God said them. I'd say it's not about the rules, but about the love."

Daniel looked at the surf. "Thanks," he said.

"Welcome," said God.

"You gonna be back around here again?" Daniel asked.

"Maybe," said God. "This is his place. I don't want to intrude too much."

"You're a good father."

"So are you."

They shook hands (for the last time on earth anyway) and Daniel started up the beach.

Abigail watched him go. She kept her eyes on the old man's back until he was out of sight. She turned back toward God. The sadness that was in her skin a moment ago was lifting.

God watched Daniel go and then turned back toward the sunrise. He closed his eyes and listened to the earth breathe. He made a mental note to tell Gabriel to find out where Zack was surfing these days. Zack should be there at the Welcome Station when Daniel arrived.

"He's a good boy," God said out loud.

Abigail looked up at him. She never felt a moment this "real" when she was alive. She didn't know if it was the new "angel" part of her or something inside her that had always been there and she just let it out. It felt good. Like that moment when you understand something you've been wrestling with. Multiply that times a hundred...a million. She stood there and finally allowed in all those lessons her parents had drilled into her as a child. All those lessons she had spent her teenage years denying...fighting. Up until now heaven had felt sort of like camp and she would be going home soon. This wasn't like camp anymore at all.

Jesus returned about 15 minutes later. God and Abigail were both sitting in their beach chairs. Abigail had her feet tucked up under her. "What's up?" Jesus asked.

"Breakfast first," God said. "Then, if you want, you can come with us on a road trip."

"Angel training?" Jesus asked.

"Something like that," God said.

Jesus was silent for a moment and then said, "Sure."

Abigail noticed there was no joy in his "Sure." More disturbing to her was the brief moment of silence before the word. It wasn't a let-me-mentally-check-my-schedule pause. It was a pause that said, "Little girl, you'd better hang on.

Chapter

6

Lorena had been working at the diner since she was 17. She had lied on her application and told the manager at the time she was 20. She told the manager her husband was killed in the war. She told the manager she had sold her wedding ring to buy the bus ticket to Florida. She told him her family had refused to approve the marriage and that was why she could not go home. She told him she was living with an aunt in a trailer park who was living on social security. She told him she was most definitely not an unwed mother. She walked in with a baby on her arm and said, "Do you have a job for someone who needs a job...today?"

The manager was a good man named Bud. He knew exactly what Lorena was when she came though the door. He said, "You ever wait tables?"

She lied. "Of course."

He said, "You ever clean a steam table or empty a grease trap?"

She lied. "I was the best at it."

He motioned her close to the counter and said quietly, "You're hired...but if you ever lie to me again after that string you just told...I'll fire you. Do we have an understanding?"

They did.

On the day after she was hired she bought a new pair of shoes for the baby with the tips she made. Bud bought a pair of good waitressin' shoes for Lorena and told her that someday she would have to return the favor to someone else.

Other than the shoes for the baby, Lorena never spent a tip in her entire career.

She and little Eddie spent a lot of time finding ways to get by. Every tip she made went toward Eddie's college fund. When Eddie was killed by the drunk driver Lorena re-named the fund "Diner Fund." And when Bud retired Lorena bought the place outright. The first thing she did as the new owner was buy every waitress a new pair of shoes.

She knew the man with the long hair. Called himself Jess. Came every once in a while. Always left a nice tip and was always kind. He walked in off the street with two new people. An older man who looked enough like Jess to be his father and a teenage girl with red hair who was most definitely not related.

They took a seat in the corner booth by the window. Jess smiled when she came over to the table.

"Good morning, Lorena," he said.

"Mornin', darlin'," Lorena said. In Lorena's Diner everyone was Sweetheart, Sugar, Love, Sweetness, Sweetsy, or Honey. If she really liked you and you came back a few dozen times...then you were Darlin'. Jesus doubted she even recognized she did this, but he considered it a promotion when it first happened.

"Lorena, this is my dad and his student Abigail," Jesus said.

Lorena smiled her best waitress smile. "Hey Sugar. Do you want to see a menu or do you...."

The father, the son, and the angel all said at the same time, "French Toast."

"Well, that was easy," she said. They all chuckled. "What would you like on it?"

Abigail said, "Blueberries. Please."

God said, "Just maple syrup."

Jesus said, "Bananas and coconut."

God and Abigail said, "Ewwww!" together.

Jesus said, "What? Oh... and maple syrup. The good stuff from the back." He winked at Lorena and she winked back.

God looked cheated. "What's the good stuff? I want the good stuff!"

Lorena shushed him. "I'll make sure you get some too. If you're Jess' daddy, you're a regular by grace."

God smiled. She collected the menus and then turned. "Be right back with coffee."

"What's the good stuff?" Abigail whispered to Jesus across the table. He smiled. "Imported. Comes from a guy named Leroy in Ohio. He makes it himself in small batches in what's left of his barn."

God was looking wistfully at the ceiling and stroking his beard. "Regular by grace." I like that.

Lorena returned with cups and then said to Abigail. "I'm sorry, Honey, what did you want to drink? I didn't even ask."

Abigail said, "Coffee is just fine, thank you. Cream?"

"I'll bring it right out." Then Lorena looked out the window and said, "Oh, here we go again."

God, Jesus and the angel all turned to see what Lorena was seeing. Two men, both in their thirties, both thin and haggard, walked toward the diner at a snail's pace. They stood on the pavement outside but did not come in.

"Homeless?" God asked.

Lorena nodded. "But it's not what you think." Lorena left the table to take the order back to the cook. The two men were soon joined by a third and then joined by a giant of an individual who towered over the others. None of them looked particularly happy. None looked very well rested. They kept their hands in their pockets and mostly seemed to whisper to each other. Eventually God saw an older man, clearly frail and dirty. He was pushing a shopping cart and using it mostly for balance. One leg seemed to be shorter than the other. He was talking to himself. He stopped the cart in front of the other men who helped him park it by the building. He protested at first; then they talked him into letting go.

Lorena returned with a vintage-looking cow creamer and set it on the table in front of Abigail. God asked, "Do they just gather up outside or do they come in?"

Lorena said, "Just watch," and then she was gone again.

A minute later an old model Honda pulled into a space and a young woman hopped out. She didn't look much older than Abigail. Around her neck was a white clerical collar. She wore a plaid skirt and a black suit jacket with an enormous Cookie Monster pin on the lapel. She seemed truly happy to see the men waiting for her. Each man received his own hug.

The giant opened the door for her and the others filed in. They had done this before. The young woman waved to Lorena who waved back but did not say anything. The men did not sit. Instead they found a place around a table on the opposite side of the diner. The first two who had arrived removed their baseball caps, followed by the giant. He nudged the frail-looking older man, who pulled off his cap and attempted to smooth his scraggly hair with his fingers.

Lorena came over to the table of men and the young woman. She placed a single cup of coffee and a plate with one donut in front of the priest.

Jesus saw it before his Father and said quietly, "Oh, wow."

Abigail said, "What?"

The young priest took a deep breath and said, "The Lord be with you."

The men quietly responded. "And also with you."

"Lift up your hearts."

"We lift them up to the Lord."

"Let us give thanks to God."

"It is right to give him thanks and praise."

The young priest said, "Amen," and the oldest member of the small group said "Amen" loudly as if he had just been woke up from a dream. One of the other men put a hand on his shoulder and a finger to his lips. The old man bowed his head again.

The priest prayed quietly the prayers that had been prayed for centuries with little variation. Prayers spoken by her grandparents, their grandparents, and their grandparents. The rhythm of words almost as comforting as the meaning beneath them.

She picked up the donut and broke it in half and said, "On the night he was arrested Jesus took the bread and said, "Take and eat this. It is my body."

She handed half of the donut to the man on either side of her. Each man broke off a piece. Each man looking as though he might just shove the whole donut into his mouth but none of them did. The priest then took the cup of coffee and she said, "This is my blood. Shed for you. Drink this and remember me." As she passed the cup around the circle each man carefully dipped his piece of pastry into the cup and then ate it.

Abigail watched the small service take place and turned to see a single tear roll down the face of the son of God. "He did the first one," she thought. "Hell, he invented this." In her head she could hear her old minister, Rev. Harmon, reading, "I am with you always." Abigail thought Rev. Harmon didn't know the half of it.

Abigail asked, "Does that count?"

God, who had been watching his son cry, put a finger to his lips. Abigail shushed until they were over. The young priest read aloud the words she had said many times. Speaking ancient prayers that took on a rhythm of their own. There was a peace in her voice. One that came from having an old soul. One that came from being in the right place at the right time and knowing it. She spoke the words as if they were lyrics to her favorite song playing on the radio as she drove with the windows down on a summer's day.

Finally Jesus said, "Does what count?"

"I mean, doesn't it have to be bread and wine or bread and juice?"

Jesus said, "I just used the leftovers from the party we had. We used to make this thing called charoset. Tasted like apple pie. Thomas was a huge charoset hound. If there had been any left of that, today Betty Crocker would be a patron saint."

God said, "It's what the food represents. Not the food itself. People get hung up on details."

Abigail said, "My church used grape juice and those little fish crackers."

Jesus nearly spit coffee through his nose and began to choke. He sputtered and coughed. Lorena came over to see if he was okay.

They heard an 'Amen' from the other side of the room. The men who were there quietly put their hats back on and filed out. The giant of a man bent low and the young priest hugged him hard. "You stay safe," she said.

As she was gathering her own things she looked up and God smiled. She smiled back. God waved her over to the table.

She came over and said, "I bet people tell you this all the time, but do you know who you look like?"

Jesus smiled. "Santa?"

"Not what I was going to say but, okay...him too."

God grinned. "Brad Pitt."

"That's the one," the priest said as if she had been thinking it all along.

God held out his hand. "My name is Avery."

"Mary," the priest said.

Jesus smiled. "That was my mother's name."

God said, "Do you do this all the time?"

"Once a week," Rev. Mary said. "I invited them to my church for the 7 am Mass, but there were those in my congregation who felt we were bringing in the wrong kind of element."

Abigail watched Jesus cringe at the idea. The youth leader at her church (she attended the youth meetings twice) showed her a verse where Jesus ate with the outcasts and the hookers. The voice that had been needling the back of her mind lately said, "See? It was true."

Jesus said, "Do you have time to join us? Can I buy you a cup of coffee?"

"Sorry," Rev. Mary said. She adjusted the larger leather briefcase on her shoulder. "I actually have a meeting at my *real* job."

God pulled his wallet out of his back pocket. It was made of duct tape. He said, "May I make a donation to your church then? Buy the next round as it were?"

"It's only a few dollars," Mary said. "I don't mind. But if you want to leave it as a tip I know Lorena is saving up for a new pie oven. Pie is proof that God exists and wants us to be happy."

The Creator of the Universe laughed out loud.

Jesus said, "It was a pleasure to meet you, Mary. I'd say 'see you in church' but I already have."

Rev. Mary smiled. It was one of the nicest things anyone had said to her. When she pulled her car out of the parking lot, Abigail turned to Jesus and asked, "Where is that verse that says you ate with the outcasts?"

Jesus said, "Uhhhhhh...."

God said, "In the book of Matthew." Then he turned to Jesus and said, "You never study."

"I was there," Jesus said.

"Still," God said, "I mean you could pick up a book once in a while."

Lorena came to the table with a tray laden with breakfast foods. When she had gone God took a fork-full and made a face like he was enraptured.

"Good?" Abigail asked.

"Wonderful!" God said. He rested his head on his hand and closed his eyes as he chewed.

"It's the syrup," Jesus said.

Abigail ate her breakfast in silence. She was lost in a memory of a similar diner in a similar place with a similar waitress, having breakfast on one of the yearly vacations her parents took her on. She remembered when she began referring to it as being "dragged on."

God watched the young angel ponder all the thoughts she was pondering and studied the light within her. She wasn't ready yet. They finished their meal and left. Jesus stopped to give Lorena a hug. She didn't notice the tip tucked under God's plate until after they were gone. Later that day there was a phone call from a bakery chain nearby. Seems they were renovating their kitchen and were wondering if there was a diner in the area that might be in the market for a used pie oven.

Chapter

God drove. Abigail sat in the back. Jesus sat in the passenger seat and played with the radio. It was an early eighties Chevy. Blue. The engine was loud but the radio was louder. God had removed his blue hooded woven pullover and tossed it in the back with Abigail. Now the Creator of the Universe sported an XXL Larry The Cucumber T-shirt. He had one hand on the wheel and one elbow on the window ledge.

Abigail leaned up and rested her head on the seat between *the* Father and *the* Son. "I have a question," she asked.

"Abigail has a question," God said to Jesus.

"I heard that someplace," Jesus said.

"What do you think the question is going to be?" God asked him.

Jesus turned around and said, "He's in a mood. He gets all feisty when he's driving. So best just to ignore him and ask your question straight up."

At that moment a large SUV blasted pass them in the passing lane. It pulled back into God's lane with less than five feet between the bumper of the SUV and the hood ornament of the Chevy. God punched the horn. The woman who was driving the SUV took her hand off the wheel (the other was holding her cell phone) and flipped the bird to God Almighty.

"Oh, that's nice!" God yelled through the windshield. "Is that why I gave you fingers?"

Abigail put her hand over her mouth and tried not to laugh. God kept going. "Real good behavior there, pregnant lady. Good parenting skills already." The SUV was already over the next rise. God simply yelled louder. "That baby just got a little uglier."

Abigail stopped laughing and looked at him. "Is she really pregnant?" Abigail asked.

God smiled. "She's on her way home with an EPT in the seat next to her. She hasn't found out yet."

Abigail said, "You didn't really make her baby uglier, did you?"

God said, "She flipped me the bird."

"She didn't know you were…you know…you."

God smiled at her in the rearview mirror. He reached up and patted her hand. "No, my dear. I did not make her baby ugly."

Jesus was still fiddling with the radio trying to find a station. God reached up and pushed his hand away and turned the dial down to the right as if he knew exactly where he wanted it.

"You're not looking for that oldies station," Jesus said.

"Driver always gets to choose the tunes," God repeated solemnly.

"Is that the lost commandment?" Abigail asked as she leaned back in the seat again.

"Shoulda been," God said. "You never had to ride with Mr. Ooo-I-just-got-the-new-Amy-Grant-CD here. Jesus looked over the back of the seat at Abigail and shrugged.

Abigail laughed.

God found the right spot on the dial just as Frankie Valli and the Four Seasons began to sing *Walk Like A Man*. Both of them hummed along until the chorus, when Jesus sang along with the bass line—"*oh bay-bee.*"

God chimed in with the falsetto and the car drifted over the next rise. Jesus reached into the glove compartment and found a pair of sunglasses. He also found an elastic band with a pink ball on the end. He held the sunglasses between his teeth as he pulled his hair into a ponytail. He slipped the sunglasses on and the two men cruised into the chorus.

Walk like a man.

Talk like a man.

Walk like a man my soooooooooooooooooon.

"Hungry?" Jesus asked.

"Not yet."

"Abby. Hungry?" God called out over the music.

"Thirsty," she said.

"Next rest stop okay?"

"That's fine."

It was the kind of abbreviated driving conversation that people have when the music is loud and the windows are down and words would just spoil the mood anyway.

They buzzed up to a car loaded with teenagers. There were three girls in the back seat, who bobbed their heads in the exact time to the music in the car that was carrying two-thirds of the Trinity. God pointed them out and pulled up beside them. Their windows were down also and they could hear the same song being belted out by a half dozen voices.

The young driver looked over and saw God singing along. He motioned for his friends to turn around and look. It was as if the cosmic tumblers of the universe had all clicked into place. Two cars, nine voices, sunshine, and an open highway.

The two cars cruised together side by side. When the song ended the driver and passengers waved and then sped away, weaving around a semi-truck ahead of them.

"They're going to get killed driving like that," Jesus said.

"Nope," God said. He was silent for a moment, and then said, "not today anyway."

Abigail sat up. "You mean they will someday."

"Some of them could," God said. "Things change."

"I couldn't do that," Abigail said.

The Lord yawned and stretched. He turned down the radio. He put his hand out the window and felt the rushing wind. "Do what?"

"Know all things at all times and not want to jump in and stop people from doing stupid things."

"Can't do it all," God said.

"You're omnipotent. You can do anything. You could have created a world that had no problems and no pain."

"Booooooooring," God said. "We've had this conversation, remember?"

"Some wouldn't think it was boring."

"Some have never had it perfect," God answered.

"You're perfect. You're not bored."

"But I got lonely," God said.

"So humanity was created 'cause you were bored?"

"I was lonely," God repeated.

"So you created pain and problems 'cause you were bored." She was goading him.

"No," God said, "I allowed *them* to create pain and problems so they would appreciate laughter and joy."

Abigail leaned up close to the front seat again. "I don't get it."

"I'm saying," God said, "that you can't have a light without a dark to stick it in."

"I don't get it."

"A world where there is no pain and everybody is happy cannot exist."

Abigail turned to Jesus. "How long have you been in Heaven?"

"Theologically speaking?" he asked.

She swatted him playfully. "Literally."

"Literally? A few thousand years."

Abigail said, "And you're not bored?"

God said, "He was human once. He died. He can appreciate it."

"But," Abigail said, "you are the one and only Lord God."

"Yes," said God.

"The great *I Am*," Abby continued.

"Yes, yes," God said. He was trying to sound humble.

"Yahweh, Jehovah...."

"Make your point," God said.

"You, the omnipotent being, Creator of the Universe, you are perfect in every way, and yet you absolutely love imperfection. Why is that?"

"I don't love imperfection," God said.

"This is what I wanted to ask you earlier," Abby said. "You can have any car you want and you choose to drive this thing. You can have angels come and sing arias in your workshop and yet you play Bob Dylan cassettes on a cheap tape player from the seventies. You love imperfection."

"I don't love imperfection." God said, "I love humanness."

"Humanness," Abigail repeated.

"My dear, there are two ways a person can go through life," God said. He put his hand back out the window again and spread his fingers wide. "Like this...." He closed his fingers, flattened his hand, and waved it up and down surfing the breeze. "Or like this."

"So being human is taking the path of least resistance?"

"No," God corrected. "Being human is choosing to take the path of least resistance or choosing not to."

Abigail leaned up over the seat and pulled a disc down from the sun visor in front of the Father of All Creation. "Hey, that's called obstructing the driver's view. That's a bad thing."

"I think I'm safe enough in this particular car," Abigail said. God looked over at his son and made a do-you-believe-this face. Jesus smiled and shrugged. "You wanted to bring her along on the road trip."

Abigail slid the disc into the CD player. Bob Dylan's voice filled the car. It was a live recording in which Bob may or may not have been aware that he was being recorded.

"HEYYYYYYYYYYYYY Mr. Tambourine man, play a song for me. I'm not sleeping and there is no place I'm going tooooooooooooo."

"So?" Abigail said. "Explain this humanness thing to me again."

"Tell her why you go to high school plays instead of Broadway," Jesus said, looking out the window.

God nodded, "I'd rather see a crooked costume sewn by a kid than a straight one sewn by an adult."

"Imperfection," Abigail said.

"Humanness," God repeated. "Any other questions?"

"Yeah," Abigail said. "Big Bang or Creationism?"

"You really want to know or are you just being facetious?"

"I want to know," Abigail said.

"You know in the Bible where it says *And God said 'Let There Be Light and there Was Light'*?"

"Yeah," Abigail said.

God smiled. "It made a hell of a loud noise."

They passed a sign for a rest stop. The words "Vending Machines" were written beneath the "miles to go."

"Soda Pop?" God asked.

"Yep," Jesus said.

"Yoo Hoo!" Abigail said.

The Almighty Jehovah pulled the Chevy into the rest area. Jesus immediately recognized the car of teens they had driven side by side with. They were all sitting on the car somewhere. Two were on the roof and the rest were on the trunk drinking soda. Abigail saw them too. "Which one?" she asked.

"Which one what?" God asked.

"Which one will take the wrong path and wind up in a car wreck?"

God was silent. He pulled the car into an empty spot near the building. The moment they left the car, one of the boys stood up and started to sing "*oh bay-bee.*"

The rest joined in on the chorus. Jesus came dancing over and took his spot with the boy doing the bass line. Abigail sang the melody with a tall blonde college student who looked like he had slept in his clothes.

God joined the girls on the "Ooooooooo-weeeeeeeee-ooooooooo," doing his best falsetto.

Strangers passed by and smiled. The sun continued to shine through a cloudless blue sky.

Six young people sang with the Son of God and His Father and a red-headed angel, though they would never know.

Chapter

A bigail floated into God's workshop. The pottery wheel was silent and the light over the drafting table was off. God was sitting by himself on the end of the couch watching TV. He was wearing a T-shirt that read, "I blessed America and all I got was this lousy T-shirt."

"You have Netflix?" Abigail asked. It had not occurred to her that she had not watched television since arriving.

"Don't need Netflix," God said. "Can watch what I want when I want to."

"Is that boring?" Abigail asked. "You already know how all the good shows are going to turn out and it's not like you can make your own stuff...not really, anyway." She settled on the couch next to the creator. She sat on the back with her stocking feet on the cushion.

"I'm not making the shows I watch, if that's what you mean," God said. "I like to see what people do with what I gave them."

A man on the screen was pacing back and forth across a massive stage. His suit looked as though it might just glow in the dark if the spotlight went out. He had a pompadour that would have made Elvis jealous, except this man's was silver—each hair combed perfectly in place and then sprayed shut. The man was doing some sort of happy-feet dance as a massive choir sang.

Oh, Jesus, Jesus is my only one.

Oh, Jesus, Jesus is my holy one.

Yes, Jesus, Jesus is the only one.

Your Jesus, Jesus is the true one.

The Jesus, Jesus is the loving one.

My Jesus, Jesus....

God hit the mute button.

Abigail said, "What do you have against seven-eleven music?"

God looked at her. "What kind of slurpees are you drinking?"

"Not Seven-Eleven," Abigail said, "although a slurpee would taste pretty good about now. I mean seven words sang eleven times."

God smiled. Abigail heard a loud hum from the other side of the workshop as a Seven-Eleven slurpee machine suddenly lit up the darkened kitchen.

Abigail smiled broadly. "What flavor?"

God said, "What flavor do you want?"

"Blue."

"Blue is not a flavor. Blue is a color."

"Ever had a slurpee?" Abigail asked.

The Creator of All Things and All Places was about to answer and then looked puzzled. "You know, I don't think I have."

"Then never mock the blue slurpee," Abigail said and zoomed toward the kitchen. "Want me to bring you one?"

"No thank you," God said, "but coffee would be nice."

Abigail opened the cupboard in the kitchen. She realized as the cupboard door opened that the shelves seemed to reach up and disappear into the clouds that should have been the ceiling. She hovered backward just slightly. "Whoa!"

From the couch, God said, "Souvenirs. I like to travel."

While the multitude of shelves seemed to have coffee mugs from various restaurants and tourist traps, the bottom shelf held only one mug. It was black with white letters that read, "Number One Dad."

Abigail floated upward. Ten, fifteen, twenty shelves up she stopped and grabbed a bright blue coffee mug. It was from Ron Jon's Surf Shop. It said so on the handle. The image on the cup looked like it came off a tacky Hawaiian shirt. She filled the Ron Jon mug with coffee and then filled the Number One Dad mug from the newly created slurpee machine, placing a bendy straw in each one.

She floated back into the room, but before she could hand the Father of All Things the blue mug she saw it was full of slurpee. The black mug was now filled with coffee. "Hey!" she said.

"Never mess with a man's favorite mug," God said. Abigail saw he had even managed to add cream. She resumed her place on the back of God's couch and let her wings hang down behind her. God noticed the wings were no longer a fashion statement, but something that was truly becoming a part of her.

The choir on TV finished and the man in the day-glo suit stopped and smiled a toothy smile. He wiped his brow with a bright white towel, which he placed under the pulpit he now stood behind.

"Friennnnnnnnnnnnnnnnnnnnnnnnnnnnnnnnnnds!" the man said.

Abigail looked at the Creator of the Universe. "Really? This is what you watch when you have the universe at your disposal?"

"Friends! I want youuuuuuu to be blesssssssed asss I have beeeeen blessssed!" He said 'blessed' with two syllables—"bless-*ed*."

One of the women in the choir called out, "Yes! Jesus!"

The man's smile grew wider, which Abigail didn't think was possible. "Frieennnnnnnnnnnnds! The Lord Goddddddd has spoken to meeeeeeee. The Lord God himmmmmmmmself has come to visit me in myyyyyyy dreeeeeeeeams."

Abigail looked at God, who shook is head. The woman who had screamed Jesus' name a moment ago seemed to lose her balance and had to be steadied by the women around her.

"Goddddd has spokennnn to meeee and told meeeee heee wants this ministryyyyyy to go onnnnn. And I want to doooo that, myyyy friennnnnnnds. I truuuuuuuuuuly do. But friends! Ministry cossssssts! We come into your home liiiiiiiiive every week. Weeee lovvvvve coming into your hooooooome every weeeeek and we are sooooooooo very thannnkfull for your inviiiitationnn. But friends! We don't just come into youuuuuuur hooome. We broadcasssssst around the worrld. Whyyyyyyyy, the electric billl for this studioooooo alone is more than myyyyyy mortgage payyyyyyment."

The crowd laughed. Abigail said, "Does he have a mortgage payment?"

God said, "He's got a mansion which includes his own private prayer garden and a prayer chapel and he writes the whole thing off."

"Now frieeeennnnds," the preacher intoned. "Our prayer partnerrrrs are standing byyyyyy right now to take youuur loooooooove offering...." God hit the mute button again. He said, "Loooooooooooser."

Abigail said, "You should call."

God chuckled. "Tell him that I think he got the message wrong?"

Abigail sat silently looking at him. God looked up and made a "you're-serious-aren't you?" face.

The angel shrugged. "What else did you have to do today."

God reached over to the small table next to the couch. The phone was lime green, circa nineteen-seventy-something. The dial had to be spun and made a loud ratchet sound as God dialed the number on the screen.

"Should I call and donate a few million and hope it's enough to get him investigated for tax fraud?"

Abigail said, "My grandmother used to watch this guy. Much as we all hated him, she really liked him. Said he made her feel like she didn't need to be afraid to die."

God asked, "How much did he soak your grandmother for?"

Abigail was about to answer, but someone on the other end of the line answered. God said, "Yes, hello? Oh hello, Missy, my telephone prayer partner."

Abigail rolled her eyes and was suddenly struck by a massive brain-freeze headache. She winced and put the heel of her palm against her eyeball. God made a "come here" motion with his hand and pushed on her forehead with his pinky. The headache was instantly gone. Abigail took another drink of her blue slurpee.

"Well, Missy, I was just wondering about something the good pastor said on my television just now.... Yes.... He said God has spoken to him in a dream. Is that true?... Oh...welll.... I see.... Yes, he must be an awfully spiritual man to have God speak to him.... You're right."

"She's sleeping with him," Abigail said, and threw her feet over the back of the couch and went to the kitchen...on foot this time. She was wearing heavy wool socks.

"Well, Missy," God said, "I'm afraid I have a slight problem

with that. See, this is God calling and I don't remember ever....
hmmmmm?... Yes, God. G-O...." He started to spell the word and
Abigail almost blew blue slurpee through her nose.

God said, "Yes, The Lord...Jehovah."

"Yahweh," Abigail offered.

"Yahweh," God said into the phone and then looked really
surprised. "I think she hung up on me."

"Nooooo!" Abigail said.

God smiled. He looked like a little kid.

Jesus walked into the room and saw his father giggling. "Oh, this
can't be good."

"He's pranking the televangelist."

"Again?" Jesus asked. He was wearing one of his many Amy
Grant concert T-shirts. This one was from 1985. He had a bottle
of sweet tea in his hand.

"You've done this before?" Abigail asked.

God looked sheepish. Jesus said, "They told him last time if he
didn't leave the good reverend alone they'd call the police."

"Let 'em try," God said, "My number is unlisted."

Abigail looked at Jesus. "Your turn."

"I'm not pranking the televangelist."

"Then call someone else."

"Who?" Jesus asked.

Abigail smiled, "Call the Elijah Christian Book and Supply Store."

Jesus looked puzzled. "Elijah was Jewish."

God handed his son the phone receiver. "Tell them that. It's ringing."

Jesus took the phone and flopped down on the couch near his father. God and Abigail heard the phone pick up on the other end. "Well, thank you," Jesus said. "I hope you are having a blessed day, too."

Jesus looked at his father as if to say, "I don't believe you made me do this." God sipped his coffee. Into the phone Jesus said, "I was just wondering. Elijah was a Jewish man, yet you have his name on your store. Do you sell Jewish items as well?"

"Ah," Jesus said. "I see. I suppose Jesus would have made him Christian before he came in."

At that moment the Father of All Life and Creator of the Universe did one of the most beautiful spit takes Abigail and ever seen—effectively spraying the coffee table and television screen with coffee. He choked and sputtered. Abigail began to slap him on the back.

"Okay," Jesus said, ignoring what was happening in front of him. "I was wondering if you have any of those gold WWJD bracelets? Oh good.... What else do you have? Uh...huh...necklaces...and earrings.... No, I guess I wouldn't wear earrings myself. Now about the earrings, is it a WW on one side and JD on the other? Because that would be confusing.... I see, all four letters on each ear. Well, you see the thing is, this is Jesus calling and I thought I might just let you know what I would do in case anyone asks.... I would.... Yes, Jesus. No...I just thought.... Excuse me?... Well now, that would not be a very Christian thing to do, would it?"

Abigail leaned in to God's ear and said, "And probably physically impossible."

God started to giggle again. He wiped the tears from his eyes with the back of his sleeve.

Jesus looked at the other two. "She hung up."

"You are just like your father," Abigail said.

Jesus hung up the phone and reached for his tea. "Gabriel said you wanted to see me about something?"

God nodded. "I think it's time for Abigail to meet you-know-who."

Abigail looked at him. "Who's you-know-who?"

Jesus said, "Oh, you know who."

Abigail, "No, I don't know who."

Jesus looked at his father. "Where does you-know-who hang about these days?"

"No idea," God said.

"No help," Jesus said.

God closed his eyes a moment. "Ah!" he said.

"Ah?" Abigail asked.

God said, "Ever been to Akron?"

***

Abigail and the Son of God walked along the sidewalk path through the flower garden. The ground and bricks were wet as if it had just rained. Abigail remembered the smell of spring. She was wearing a black dress. Jesus was in a pair of dark khaki pants and a button-down shirt. Abigail realized it was the first time she had seen him in something other than an Amy Grant concert T-shirt.

There were a few dozen people all quietly walking in along the path. They spoke in whispered quiet voices. Abigail said, "Can they see me?"

"Sort of," Jesus said.

"What do you mean sort of?"

"I mean you look like a teenage girl walking into a church. No one is going point and say, 'Look Mom, an angel.'"

"Will I show up in photographs or in mirrors?"

"This ain't *Twilight*," Jesus said, keeping his voice low.

"*Twilight* vampires sparkle," Abigail said. She looked around at the other people and realized she was being too happy. Nobody else was smiling.

"Where are we?" she said changing her tone.

"Come with me a sec." Jesus took her by the hand and led her around to the back of the church building. "Wait for it," he said.

Something happened in the next moment that Abigail did not have words for. Suddenly she knew they were not alone...but it was more than a "not alone" feeling. It was more of a not at *all* alone. Completely and totally not alone. It was more than a someone-one-else-is-here feeling. It was a completeness.

"Spook," Jesus said.

Abigail turned to see what Jesus was looking at and saw...saw...a something.

Imagine you are looking at a person. You are looking them square in the face. They are standing right in front of you. Now imagine they are gone, but the shadow of them remains. The shadow their nose makes against their face. The shadows in the creases of the lines around their eyes. As if you were drawing a person and started with the shading. This is what Abigail saw in front of her.

"Abigail, this is the companion," Jesus said. There was something in his voice that said "All kidding is over." But he wasn't at all serious. He seemed to be happy about the meeting.

Abigail squinted as if maybe she might make out who this companion was. Then, like a breeze, the companion passed completely through her. Abigail gasped. She was overwhelmed by a rapid series of senses.

As if she were smelling pancakes and maple syrup....

And holding her grandmother's hand at the Thanksgiving table....

And the taste of Milo's Sweet Tea on a hot August day....

And the view from the top of the roller coaster....

And the harmonies of the "Ahhhhhhhhhhhhh" in the opening of Eleanor Rigby....

And the feel of sand between her toes....

And the sound of the baseball bat connecting at a ball game....

And the dimming of the lights just before the movie you've been waiting all year to see....

And the touch of a blankie (not a blanket but a blankie)....

And the smell of donuts when you open the door of the shop early in the morning....

And rain when you don't care if it's raining....

And when the unexpected package arrives with your name on it....

And walking around on Halloween with your new costume and plastic bucket....

And the first snowfall....

And the last day of school....

And ice cream....

And a thousand other senses all occurring at the same moment. They enveloped her and then faded just as quickly as the companion passed through her back.

Abigail said, "Whoa!"

Jesus said, "Yeah. Companion likes you."

Abigail's eyes got wider. "Trinity part three?"

"If you want to think about it that way...I guess that's close enough," Jesus said.

"Why haven't I met companion before?"

Jesus said, "The companion exists here. The companion is God's presence on earth."

Abigail's mind started to reel. The questions began building up in her head like rubber bouncy balls being poured off the roof of a tall building. She tried to grab at any of them.

The companion passed through her again. This time it was like calm waters, the sound of beach waves, cool evening breezes, the smell of autumn leaves, dark coffee...and Abigail breathed deep.

She looked around, but the sense they were not alone was gone. They were, in fact, by themselves, standing at the back of the church.

"And what was that about?" she asked.

Jesus took her hand again and said, "Come with me."

They quietly took their place in the line of people slowly making their way into the church building. There were flowers along both sides of the steps into the church sanctuary. Many flowers. A huge wreath of lilies seemed to be wedged awkwardly near the door as if it had been a last minute edition.

Abigail accepted the paper bulletin from the older man in the black suit at the back of the sanctuary. His suit was so perfect she imagined he worked at the funeral home.

Abigail looked at the cover of the simple folded paper. It showed a young man, perhaps in his twenties. He wore a white shirt and tie, which did not look normal on him. The picture had obviously been clipped from a larger picture. Abigail wondered about who else had been in the photo.

Jesus led her to the pew furthest in the back. It was a sort of half-pew, its back against the wall. A man was already seated there. Jesus and Abigail sat, with the Son of God in the middle. They were quiet as the organ played an agonizingly slow rendition of *How Great Thou Art.*

The other man in the half-pew put his face into his palm and said quietly, "I hate this song. She knows I hate this song."

Abigail looked at the man sitting there and then, almost calmly, looked at the photo on the front of the bulletin. She sat back against the pew and said, "Whoa."

Jesus said, "This is Edgar. It's his funeral."

"I wasn't expecting you," Edgar said, though he did not look at Jesus. "I was waiting for demons to drop down out of the ceiling."

"Hollywood," Jesus said, shaking his head.

"I'm going to hell, aren't I?" Edgar said. He did not seem surprised.

Jesus said, "After all the time we spent building you a new bike? Not hardly."

Edgar closed his eyes. He seemed relieved. "But I had to stick around for this part?"

"Be a shame to miss it," Jesus said. "All those people saying nice things about you. They should do this before you die."

"I wasn't all that nice," Edgar said. "You, my sacred friend, are about to hear a series of well-thought-out, carefully worded crap...and I don't know half these people."

"They came for your mom and sister," Jesus said. "They go to this church."

"I didn't go to church...." Edgar said. Then added, "Much."

Jesus smiled, "First time I went back to my hometown church my mother had invited the entire community and after I preached they tried to throw me off a cliff."

Edgar chuckled. "Is that really true?"

"Swear to God."

Abigail began to laugh and then turned it into a quiet cough.

Edgar said, "Who's your friend?"

Jesus said, "This is Abigail."

"Hello," Abigail said. It came out a lot more cheery than she wanted it to.

"Is she one of those happy-happy-joy-joy types?" Edgar asked.

Jesus rolled his eyes. "Like hanging out with a box of Lucky Charms."

Abigail nudged him in the ribs. She was going to explain to Edgar that she was not a box of Lucky Charms; she was, in fact, dark and cynical and sardonic. But when she looked at Edgar she could not bring herself to say it. The fact was, she hadn't felt all that dark and cynical and sardonic in quite a while.

The organist finished the hymn and Edgar seemed to breathe a sigh of relief. An older man in a black robe stood up and cleared his throat. His voice was clear and held a deep wisdom, as if he had done this many times before and knew he would probably do it many more. His voice held a stability and a calmness that Abigail latched onto immediately. She felt a strong sense of sympathy for everyone in the room, including the priest and the man sitting on the other side of Jesus.

The minister prayed. The congregation said, "Amen."

A woman stood up from her place next to a grieving woman in black. Edgar said, "I seemed to have made a habit out of making my mother cry." Jesus leaned over and gave the man a supportive nudge—a manly version of a pat on the knee.

The woman, who bore a striking resemblance to a weeping woman in the first pew, took a deep breath.

"My sister," Edgar said. "She can really sing."

The organist began to play, much softer this time, and it was as if the entire room breathed in with the singer as she began.

Amazing Grace! How sweet the sound
That saved a wretch like meeeeeeeeeeeeeeeeee.

The woman's voice was pure and lovely and seemed to float out of her as if it was the most natural thing in the world.

"Whoa," Abigail said. She realized she'd been saying that a lot lately.

"Toldya," Edgar said, leaning forward with his elbows on his knees. He was watching his baby sister and smiling as if they were at a high school talent show.

I once was lost, but now I am found.
Was blind, but now I see.

Edgar suddenly sat up as if he just now understood a complicated math formula.

"My God! This song is about me, isn't it?"

Jesus watched the man who had just recently wrapped his motorcycle around the tire of a semi-truck sit in wonder of the moment.

'Twas grace that taught my heart to fear
And grace my fears relieved.
How precious did that grace appear
The hour I first believed.

A ray of sunlight came through the church window. It bathed the room in color. Abigail saw that no one else seemed to be reacting to it and wondered if it was real. She saw the companion, or rather didn't see it, or rather saw what it wasn't...or was. She really didn't understand, but felt caught up in the moment. The companion floated above Edgar's sister as she sang. The companion was spinning.

Through many dangers toils and snares
I have already come.
'Twas grace that brought me safe thus far
And grace shall lead me home.

The companion seemed to soar away from the singer and up into the rafters of the church. Abigail watched it move. Then it lowered and began to dance across the top of the congregation. Lightly, gently, on top of one person and then another. Each person seemed to draw into themselves and then quietly begin to weep. Purses were opened. Kleenex was shared. Hankies were pulled from inner suit coat pockets. Eyes were wiped.

When we've been there ten thousand years,
Bright shining as the sun

The singer's voice lifted and began to bounce off the walls. The organist stopped and buried her face in her own hands, overcome. The singer refused to quit despite the tears in her own eyes.

We've no less days to sing God's praise
Than when we first begun.

Abigail watched the companion dance to the sweet a capella voice and leap effortlessly from one side of the room to the other, pushing itself off the walls and and soaring like a breeze over the room.

Amazing grace! How sweet the sound
That saved a wretch like me.

Edgar hung his head and began to cry. Jesus put a hand on Edgar's back and let him weep.

I once was lost, but now I am found,
Was blind, but now I see.

It was as if that was the moment Edgar's sister realized the organist had stopped. She turned to see the musician trying to regain her composure, but the song was over.

Edgar sat up and ran his hands through his hair as if he were pushing away bits of pain and grief and sadness. The light that only the three in the back pew saw slowly faded.

Edgar turned his wet eyes to Jesus and whispered, "If it's all the same to you, I think I'm ready to leave."

Jesus nodded and gave Edgar another reassuring pat on the back.

No one seemed to notice as the trio stood and left.

Chapter

God stood just outside of the Welcome Station. He was pacing back and forth, almost nervous. He wore his white suit. His long white hair was combed and pulled back. He had even given his beard a trim—which was unnecessary. But he wanted to feel as though he was sprucing up.

Abigail, who had been told simply to "look nice for this," was in her favorite dress. It was the one she had on earth the Easter before. She had picked it out herself—the first time shopping for a nice Easter dress without the mother intervention. Her wings were white this time, the tattoo hidden discreetly under the sleeve of the dress. She had no idea why she was here. And yes, she was fully aware of the other angels looking out the windows of the Welcome Station at her. Why did *she* get to be the one to stand outside with God?

Jesus arrived and he was practically vibrating. "Is she here?"

God turned and looked at his son. The cargo pants were matched by the Summer Park Vacation Bible School 1982 T-shirt. God raised an eyebrow. Jesus said, "What? She designed this shirt. It's one of my favorites."

Abigail looked at the shirt. Just below the VBS title was a color drawing of what appeared to be St. Peter and St. Paul running childlike side by side. Peter had a balloon and Paul had a picnic basket.

Jesus said, "You. You look like you're selling ice-cream."

God's white suit turned to a CEO gray. "Better?" he asked. At that moment the distant horizon began to glow. It became so bright that Abigail could not see either of the two men to her left and right. She held her hand up to shield her eyes. The light grew brighter and then suddenly vanished. In the distance a small figure stood looking around, as if she had no idea what was happening.

Abigail leaned in closer to God's son. "Who is that?"

"That," Jesus said, "Is Ms. Frankie."

Abigail squinted. Ms. Frankie was a small woman. She leaned heavily on a cane and took small steps toward the Welcome Station. Abigail said to the Creator, "You didn't want to send a car or something?"

God did not take his eyes off the frail figure coming toward them. "She doesn't need the cane," God said. "It's habit. She'll figure out in a little while that her hip doesn't hurt and neither do her hands."

God stood up a little straighter, almost at attention. Abigail asked, "And who is Ms. Frankie?"

God smiled as if he loved to tell this story. "Ms. Francine Davidson is the director of Christian Education at the Summer Park Community Church. She took the job when she was 19 years old. She was 96 on her last birthday."

Jesus put in, "She did not retire."

God nodded. "She did not retire. When she was 25, a boy in the street outside her church was hit by a bullet during a gang fight. The child lay there in the street as a bunch of thugs continued to shoot at each other from the curb and apartment windows. Ms. Frankie walked out into the middle of the street and scooped the boy up into her arms and walked with him into a store. When the ambulance said they would not come to that part of the city she carried the boy 12 blocks to a clinic."

Jesus continued the tale. "When she was still in her twenties she began a program to offer free breakfast to students in her district. Her own church was not on the path to school, so she asked a church that was nearby to let her feed children before school. They said no. So she bought a tent and set it up just outside of the school gate and fed kids breakfast every day until the community pressed other local churches to take it over."

God said, "Tell her what happened when she was sixty."

Jesus laughed out loud. "When Ms. Frankie was 60, a man tried to grab a little girl from the playground outside her church. Ms. Frankie spotted him. He thought he could easily take down a short sixty-year-old woman."

God offered, "Who had two black belts in judo."

Jesus repeated, "Who had two black belts in judo. She put a high heel in the man's forehead and then put a knee in his back until the police arrived."

"She has given her entire life to this service," God said. She gave seven years working overseas in an AIDS clinic for children. No child in her care has gone unfed, uneducated, or unloved."

Both men stood a little straighter. Abigail said, "Shoulda had a band."

God and Jesus looked at each other as if to say "I thought *you* were getting the band."

As the small figure got closer, the two men moved forward. Abigail stood where she was. This moment was theirs. They were meeting their hero.

Jesus opened his arms. "Francine, welcome."

Ms. Frankie, barely five feet tall, received Jesus' hug and wrapped her arms around his waist. She ran her ancient trembling finger along the scars in his wrists and gently kissed each one.

She turned toward God. He smiled and opened his arms. "Ms. Francine, I want you to know...."

Then something unexpected happened. To say it was unexpected says a *lot* considering who it was about to happen to.

The small frail woman reached up and grabbed God's necktie and pulled. The Creator of the Universe, being attached to it, followed. Frankie pulled him down so they were almost nose to nose. In a voice so quiet it was almost a whisper she asked, "Why?"

"Excuse me?" God asked.

Frankie said it again louder this time. "Why?" There was so much emotion in her voice it was impossible to comprehend it all. The sadness of seeing children die, the wisdom of nearly a century of studying scriptures, a lifetime of experience, the combination of sweet relief and complete exhaustion...

...all of it was in that one word. *Why?*

"They are children. They are *your* children. How can you let them die?" She released her grip on his tie and he stood up again. Tucking his tie back into his vest, he composed himself. In all his years, which technically was *all* of the years, he had never been asked that as a first question. Not since Job had he been so profoundly called on the carpet.

"Frankie," God said, "come with me." He held out his hand and the old woman took it. She turned around as a mother would look for a lost child and held out her other hand for the savior. Jesus took it and the trio walked along the path. Abigail, still unbelieving what she had just seen, floated behind them.

The Father, the Son, the teacher and the angel all traveled down a long path. Abigail noticed that Ms. Frankie wasn't limping anymore. She wondered if Frankie noticed she wasn't limping anymore.

As they crested a small hill they stood and looked down at a playground. It was unlike anything that had ever been seen or built on earth. A playground unencumbered by committee rules and regulations...a playground unencumbered by the laws of physics. A thousand children giggled and screamed as they ran from one ride to another. The seesaw was twenty yards long. A dozen children sat on either end. A merry-go-round spun so fast that the children seemed to cling on for life, but they shouted with the joy of moving so fast. A set of climbing bars stretched from one end of the playground to the other. Neither end seemed to be fastened to the ground. It was a great expanse of metal floating in the air. The slide was a mile long and a mile high. Each time a child slipped or fell an angel appeared instantly and placed the small hands back on the bars. Still, with all the amazing rides, there were still children playing jump rope and tag and every imaginable playground game. There were children in Victorian dress and others in animal skins. None of it mattered. All of it was joy. Pure unadulterated joy.

Off to the side of the merry-go-round was an angel dressed in a blue jumper and a yellow T-shirt. She was sitting cross-legged with a group of six or eight little girls. They were playing jacks. The angel would dip her gigantic wings and make a breeze. The girls would giggle and reach up for the white feathers, which would lift up just out of their reach, and they would giggle again. The angel looked up and saw the trio standing up on the hill. God nodded at a small girl in an African dress. She nodded back and gently took the little girl's hand. She formed the hand into a pointer and then began to spin it around like a divining rod. The girl giggled at the new game. Eventually the angel steered her pointing finger to the top of the hill and the girl saw the trio.

"Frankie!" she said. Her smile widened to an amazing size. Her teeth were white and healthy. Her eyes were clear and free of infection. She came running toward the woman she had loved so much.

Frankie kneeled and received the child into her arms. "I died," said the little girl.

"I know you did," said Frankie. "I was with you."

"I saw you there," the girl said. "You were crying. My mother was crying. I wanted to stay, but this pretty lady came and said we had to leave." The girl threw her arms around her old friend again.

Little by little, one by one, other children began to notice the visitors. Jesus, who came here often, immediately found some familiar friends and raced them to the top of the monkey bars. Two little boys ran to the angel, who scooped each one up and then floated with them to the top of the hill. The boys shook with glee.

Frankie recognized each face as it came before her. She had lost so many. She had lost count of how many. Now all these bright faces came back to her. They all had been so sick when she'd seen them last. Now, they were all bright and healthy. They lived in a world of pure joy.

God stood and watched and waited while the newest arrival received a thousand embraces and a thousand kisses. The children she knew introduced her to others. Faces of all colors kissed the old friend of their playmates. Soon the crowd thinned and each of the smiling faces returned to the wondrous world of play, one small group of them shepherded by the wings of an angel.

Jesus said good-bye to his friends and climbed down. He accepted a few hugs on his way back to where the teacher and his father were waiting.

"I didn't allow them to suffer, Frankie," God said. "I allowed their suffering to end. I took them away from the pain and brought them to this place."

"I know," Frankie said. She was still on her knees watching the children. "I was so angry at you."

"There aren't enough people on the earth like you," God said, coming closer. "If there were more like you, then there would be more playgrounds and fewer cemeteries." He held out his hand. She took it and rose, then realized that she didn't need the help. The pain in her body was gone. The weariness was gone.

"Do you want to see your house?" Jesus said. "We've had people working on it for years. It's just on the other side of the playground. It's got a porch so you can come out and watch any time."

"Watch?" Frankie said. "I want to try out the monkey bars."

Jesus looked at her and smiled. He took her hand and the two of them ran into the throng of a thousand laughing children.

Chapter

10

For as long as he could remember Thomas had lived in a fog. Sometimes…most of the time…he had to work hard to stay focused on what was going on around him. His elementary school teachers had called him a daydreamer—something his father had attempted to knock out of him by knocking some sense into him.

Thomas had no name for "the other place." It wasn't even a "place" really. It was just a way that Thomas let his mind "go." When Thomas was in "the other place" his body just seemed to move on its own and make its own decisions. Thomas liked "the other place." Words didn't hurt him there. Grades were no longer a problem. People who picked on him…bullied him… were nothing any more. He was simply "away" and it was better. So after 17 years of struggling…of people telling him to shape up, grow up, and just snap out of it…Thomas gave himself completely over to "the other place."

Thomas knew where his father kept the guns. Sometimes when he was "away" Thomas could watch out of his own eyes when his hands played with his father's weapons. They were in the back of the closet in a gray box. When he was small he stood on a chair to reach them. (He had been looking for Christmas presents.) Now he went there a few times a month when everyone was out of the house.

He loaded them and put them in his backpack and walked in late to school. He heard the girls giggling in the hallway around the corner. He dropped the bag and pulled out the guns and was ready when they turned and saw him. They both started to scream at the same time. He stopped the one almost instantly. The explosion was so loud that he had to stop and look at the gun. He had never heard it fire before. His wrist hurt. He wondered if he'd sprained it. He wondered if he was holding the gun wrong.

The other girl had run.

The screams and the shots brought dozens more into the hallway, including the teachers.

Mr. Harper said, "Thomas." He said it the way he used to say it in class when he saw Thomas not paying attention. Thomas shot him in the chest.

Thomas poked his head in the room and fired two random shots. One, he was pretty sure, hit a guy in the shoulder. He didn't see where the other one went. He shot lockers and the drinking fountain and the window of the home economics class. The custodian came running toward him with a wrench and Thomas shot him too.

Soon they were all hiding and crying. Thomas was hunting. It took four minutes for the police to arrive. It took them thirty seconds after that to find Thomas. It took Thomas only a second to point the pistol at the police officer. It took a heartbeat to stop Thomas cold.

Thomas was sleeping on the couch in God's room. It was raining outside. God wore his blue hooded sweatshirt and sat in his recliner drinking coffee. Jesus sat at the table with his feet propped up on the chair across from him. He was reading the new book Mark Twain had recently finished.

Abigail stood in the kitchen with her wings folded tightly behind her. She wasn't aware of it then, but she was standing as physically far away as she could from the boy on the couch and still be in the same room. She sipped her Yoo-Hoo. She'd brought a coffee to God and one to the Savior, both times walking the long way around the living room set, so as not to get too near. Now she looked outside at the rain. She wanted to ask how it could be raining when they were so far above the clouds but she simply decided that if God wanted to hear rain on the window then it was going to rain on the window. She inhaled deeply and smelled the rain. It was a spring rain. She remembered being able to tell the difference even as a child. "Spring rain has sunshine in it," she had once told her mother. He mother thought that was very cute and told her grandmother what little Abigail had said.

"Should we wake him?" Jesus asked.

"No," God said. He leaned his head back against the cushion on the recliner and listened to the rain. As if he was reading Abigail's thoughts he said, "Rain was such a good idea. I love the smell of it. It seems so refreshing."

"It was raining when I died," Jesus reminded him. "And when you destroyed the earth."

"I was angry," God said.

"I like Spring rain," Abigail said. "Sometimes it would rain in October before it started to get cold. My mother would shut the window. But she always opened it up for Spring rain."

Jesus looked up at her. "You know in the area where I was born, there was no word for 'bad rain'?

"Really?" Abigail asked.

"Every rain was a good rain no matter what it was," Jesus said. My step-father used to dance in the rain. He and the other men would put down their tools and go outside. I used to sit under his workbench and laugh. My mother would yell at them from the window but they would just keep right on dancing.

God sipped his coffee and looked at the boy on the couch. "Pity."

"It really is a fine line, isn't it?" Abigail said. She still hadn't come out of the kitchen, but she didn't take her eyes off the sleeping boy who wasn't that much younger than she was.

"Abigail, my dear, you can come in here. Thomas isn't going to hurt anyone."

"He makes me uncomfortable."

God nodded. "I understand. But I don't want to yell because he's sleeping. Would you come and sit with us?"

Abigail waited a moment and then brought her Yoo Hoo into the living room and sat on the overstuffed chair opposite God. Jesus dog-eared the page and looked at her. "You were saying."

Abigail kept looking at the boy. Asleep, he seemed like he was two years old. "I said it's a fine line."

"How's that?"

"Well, sometimes you get directly involved and change things. Other times you let things go."

God was quiet for a moment. "All things happen for a reason. Sometimes I have to give them a nudge. Sometimes things just happen on their own. Sometimes it's like picking up the pieces after someone dropped the Star Wars glass."

"The what?" Abigail asked.

God smiled. "The Star Wars glass. There was a fast-food chain that came out with these cool Star Wars drinking glasses after the first movie came out in the 70's. I had the whole set. One day I knocked my Darth Vader glass off the counter and it shattered. Seemed like it shattered more than any other regular glass would, but I guess that was because it was irreplaceable."

"But you could replace it," Abigail said. "If you wanted ten Darth Vader glasses you could have them. Ten cases."

"Can't replace it," God said. "I broke it. All I could do was clean it up so nobody would cut themselves."

"I don't get it." Abigail said.

"It's all part of a concrete plan that's constantly adjusting," Jesus said.

Abigail said, "But you can't build a house if someone changes the blueprints every time a nail is driven."

"Tell me about it," God said. Abigail flopped back against the chair and scowled.

Thomas stirred on the couch. The first thing he did was smell the rain. It was a clean Spring rain. Thomas pulled the afghan up around his shoulders and buried his face deeper into the flannel pillowcase. Slowly he opened one eye and then the other.

God placed his cup on the table next to his chair. It was a blue cup that said *World's Greatest Abba* on the side. Abigail had given it to him on Father's Day a few months ago. "Thomas?" God said.

Thomas lifted his head. He was still in the fog, but not really. He immediately tried to retreat back to the faraway place, but he couldn't. He pushed up with his hand and swung his feet around to the floor. He pulled the blanket around his shoulders and rubbed his eyes. If he was curious or puzzled about where he was, he didn't show it.

"Are you cold?" God asked.

Thomas nodded. God looked over at Abigail, who stood up, went over to the window and closed it. She leaned against the wall and looked at Thomas.

"Thomas, do you know where you are?" God asked.

Thomas looked around, still drowsy, and licked his lips. Thomas shook his head.

God said, "Thomas, you've done something that wasn't good. You don't remember it now. In a minute, I'm going to let you remember what you did and you probably won't feel very well. Do you understand?"

Thomas tried harder to let his brain go to the other place but he couldn't.

Jesus walked over toward Thomas. "Stand up here, big guy." Jesus' tone was friendly but serious.

Thomas stood. He was the same height as the Savior. Jesus looked at his Father, who nodded. Jesus reached out and brushed the hair from Thomas face. That was all it took.

Thomas' mind cleared. For the first time ever he could think without it hurting. The fog was gone. He didn't have to work to focus on what was going on around him. It was a clarity that he hadn't known before. It was like pulling your head out of a rubber Halloween mask, only it happened with his soul. He started to smile.

Then he remembered.

He remembered everything.

"Oh," Thomas said, and doubled over as if he may vomit. But he didn't. "Ohhh," he said, this time looking up and seeing Jesus and understanding fully where he was. He looked around the room as if he were searching for a door. He tried to throw the blanket off, but it caught on his finger. Thomas began to shake his hand as if he were trying to flick something gross off it. "No no no no no no no no no," he repeated over and over. Freeing himself from the blanket, he collapsed on the floor and started to weep.

"Ahh... Ahhhh... Ahhh..." Thomas said as the tears began to run down his cheeks. "I didn't mean it!" he said.

Jesus bent down and with no more effort than it takes to lift a rag doll he lifted the crying young man and held him against his chest.

Thomas wept for the years he had lost. He wept for all the horrible things his father had done to him to "make him snap out of it." He wept for all the people he could have known. He wept for all the people he had hurt. With each sob the rain pounded harder against the glass, but Thomas was not aware of this. Abigail was.

He clutched Jesus' sleeve and soaked his T-shirt with tears. He cried like a baby. He had no memory of ever crying before. If something hurt, he could just send his mind away and it didn't hurt anymore. Now there was no place to go. So he cried and cried and cried.

Finally he looked at Jesus. "The others...from the school?"

"Some of them are here," God said. "Some will be along later."

Thomas' feet were still not supporting him. Jesus was holding him in place. Holding him in an embrace that felt more secure than Thomas could ever remember feeling.

"Am I going to Hell?" Thomas asked.

"No," God said, standing. He put his hand on Thomas' back. "I think you're just coming out of it."

God reached over and lifted Thomas under the arms and stood him on his feet. The boy wiped his eyes and nose with his sleeve.

"I'm I'm I'm so..so..sorry," Thomas said, on the verge of crying again.

"I know," God said.

"I'd like to lay down again," Thomas said.

Jesus laid the boy back on the couch and covered him with the afghan. Thomas started to cry again and was soon asleep.

God looked at the boy for a long time. "Are the others still outside?"

Jesus nodded.

God looked at Abigail. "Will you tell them to wait a while, please?" God asked.

Abigail looked surprised. "What should I say?"

"Tell them they are home. Tell them Thomas is sleeping. He'll be out in a little while."

"I don't know how to tell them that," Abigail said. Her wings, which had loosened up slightly during their conversation, now clenched up again.

"I'll go with you," Jesus said. He took her hand and they started toward the door.

"Abigail?" God said.

The young angel turned, but she didn't meet his eyes.

"Give me a little bit and then you and I will have a chat. Okay?"

Jesus and the angel left the room. God sat back down in his chair and picked up his coffee. The window behind him opened just a little on its own and the Lord inhaled deeply. He sipped his coffee quietly and listened to the sound of the rain.

Chapter

When God wandered into the other room with his coffee he saw Abigail pacing back and forth, taking angry steps. Her wings were open but not spread. She was so angry that her feathers were vibrating.

"You can punch the wall if you want to, Abigail," God said. "You can't hurt yourself or the wall. People used to say that thunder was just the sound of God bowling, but to tell you the truth it was me punching the wall whenever I got fed up."

Abigail did not smile. She did not punch the wall. She did not stop pacing.

"How did they take it?" God asked.

"How do you think they took it?" Abigail said. "Why, I bet they were a little upset."

"They'll get over it."

"That's it?" Abigail shouted. She was only vaguely aware that she was shouting at God. "They'll get over it? They get up and go to school and some idiot decides to take guns with him and they don't get to go home tonight?"

"They are home," God said.

"That's not what I mean and you know it."

"What do you mean?" God asked.

"I mean that they're here and down there someplace there's a wife and there's a mother and there's a boyfriend and there's a whole bunch of people who are going to be sending up some really pissed-off prayers tonight. You might want to take them to see the fountain of prayers. I'm sure it will be really pretty."

She stopped pacing and looked at him. "I want to ask you something."

"Okay."

"That day in your workshop when you were working on Roy's life."

"I remember."

"I asked if I there was a vase of me and you said, 'there was.'"

God nodded.

"What happened to it?" Abigail asked.

"You broke it."

"*I* broke it? *Me*?"

"I didn't break your vase, Abigail."

"You said it was a joint project."

"It was," God said. "Every clay vase has to go through the fire. Yours didn't make it."

"You could just fix everything. You could just look down and make people happy."

"What would be the point?" God asked.

"Nobody wants to hurt," Abigail said.

"No," God said, "but there are such things as sorrow, as grief, as pain. These are part of life."

"But they shouldn't be," Abigail said. She felt like she was getting smaller...heavier.

"Of course they should be," God said. "If you have never been face down in the filthy parking lot...you can't appreciate the dance."

"What is that?" Abigail asked. "A T-shirt from the Christian bookstore?"

"I think it might be closer to Buddha," God said.

Abigail crossed her arms and held herself tightly. "People don't want to feel hurt."

God said, "Neither does a bowl of vanilla ice cream."

Abigail looked at him. "What?"

God said, "You can go through your life never taking risks and blaming everyone for your problems and never putting yourself out there, but then you're just vanilla."

Abigail said, "What about French Vanilla?"

"It's *still* vanilla," God said. "Notice the name."

Abigail said, "I like vanilla."

God said, "No you don't. You like all the gooey and crunchy stuff. You like swirls and fudge and nuts."

She turned away from him and said, "Then vanilla was all that I was offered."

God shrugged. "Could have gone out and gotten some of the good stuff."

"Not when you are stuck in a house with a bunch of vanilla people."

"Abigail," God said. "Everything is a choice. Who you are is not because your mom smoked, your daddy drank, your best friend is prettier or your teacher doesn't think you have talent. Who you are is who you *choose* to be."

Abigail was pacing again. "If it's my choice, why do you have clay under your fingernails?"

God sipped his coffee. "I told you. It was a joint project."

"It didn't feel like it."

"Don't pee on my leg and tell me its raining, Abigail. You made a really stupid choice."

"You didn't stop me.

God looked surprised. "Is that what you were waiting for?"

Abigail gestured around the room like a prize girl on a game show. "I'm here now. I'm in heaven. Everlasting paradise. The earthen vessel is no more. And now I can shine. Sounds like a good choice to me."

God looked at her. "When I told you about the vases, you said you don't feel like a treasure."

Abigail said, "It's better than what I had."

God cocked his head. "Are you sure?

"I hated my life."

God came toward her slowly. "Abigail, you'll never be able to appreciate what's up here until you can appreciate what you left behind."

"I did what I did because I wanted to."

God set his coffee mug down on a table. "Like I said, a very stupid choice."

Abigail was holding herself again. "What was my other choice? A life as vanilla?"

"You knew there was more."

"I did not." Her voice cracked slightly and she thought maybe God had not heard it. But she knew he had.

"You wanted it so bad you could taste it," God said. "You wanted to explode."

Abigail pulled herself in tight. "If I had wanted to stay I'd still be there."

"Are you sure?"

"Yes," she said coldly.

God said, "Do you remember what happened after you took the pills?"

"I died."

"Between taking the pills and dying. Do you remember what you did?

"I was lying there on my bed."

"How do you know?

Abigail was looking at the wall even though God was close enough to touch. "'Cause I remember seeing myself."

"Seeing yourself?"

"Yes."

"From the outside."

"It was from the outside. I was standing next to my bed looking at myself."

The Father of All Creation allowed the young angel to experience the memory fully and then he asked her quietly, "Then what happened?

Abigail looked at his ancient eyes and felt every part of her soul start to crumble like a sand castle beneath a wave of sorrow. "I…I…I changed my mind."

"You did?"

Abigail was crying now. "I kept yelling at myself to wake up… wake up. I kept yelling it, but she didn't move. Oh…I changed my mind!"

The being who had been around since before there was time opened his arms and the angel walked into them. God wrapped himself around her. He wrapped "himself" around her. She cried into his sweatshirt.

"I changed my mind. I changed my mind. I changed my mind. I changed my mind." She said it over and over again.

God allowed her to cry against him. He rocked slowly back and forth and said, "Shhhhhhhhhhhh."

Abigail said, "I miss my mom" into the folds of blue cotton.

"I know," God said soothingly.

Abigail said, "I miss my dad and I miss Ben & Jerry's."

God held her and stroked her hair.

"I changed my mind. I changed my mind. I changed my mind." She said it until it was unintelligible.

Jesus walked into the room and saw his Father embracing the angel. He made a motion as if to say "Everything okay?"

God gave him a thumbs-up.

"I'm sorry. I'm sorry. I'm sorry. I'm sorry. I'm sorry."

"For what, child?" God asked.

"For breaking my vase."

God held her tighter.

"Why didn't you send me to hell?" she asked.

God lifted her from his chest. Her hands were trembling and her face tear-stained. He looked into her young eyes with his ancient ones. "Because I love you," he said.

"And there's no air conditioning," Jesus said.

Abigail stood up. "I'm sorry. I didn't know you were there."

Jesus smiled. He was wearing another Amy Grant concert T-shirt. He reached into his pocket and pulled out a ticket. "Listen," he said. "Mozart is back in town. He and John Lennon have this really cool duet act. Bunch of us are going. I've got an extra ticket."

"I don't think so," Abigail said.

"We'll stop for ice cream afterward." Jesus waved the ticket in front of her.

She smiled. Then she wrapped her arms around the great I Am, the Almighty, the great Jehovah, and she took the ticket from his son and they went out the door together.

God watched them go and walked over to the pottery wheel. He grabbed his leather apron from a hook on the wall. He tied it behind him and flipped the switch and listened to the hum of the motor. He looked up at the shelves of vases. Shelf after shelf. Higher and higher until they disappeared into the night sky.

Chapter

(12)

Abigail could hear the Father softly humming from "the picture room." It was a small windowless room. It could not have been more than 15 feet square but the walls were so tall that the human eye could not detect their peak. Which is just as well since no human had ever been in the picture room. There was no door. None was necessary. Though God often copied the designs from earth for places in heaven (or was it visa versa?) he had no need of anything physical. Walls, floors, windows, and doors were all a matter of choice.

The walls were covered with drawings of the Creator. Each one was created by a child. Each one hung in an ornate gold frame. Sometimes God brought children who had died to the picture room and showed them where he had hung their artwork. It made them remember that they were special.

Abigail appeared next to God. There was no "poof" or fancy effect. One moment she wasn't there and the next she just "was."

God was painting. He wore a blue painter's smock that looked as though it had not been washed since the dawn of time. He wore a Cleveland Indians baseball cap backward on his head. He had once owned an artist's beret, but every time Gabriel saw him in it, the angel would chuckle and then pretend he hadn't. God had gotten tired of listening to Gabriel fake a cough and leave the room.

Abigail held two bottles of ice tea in her hands and she offered one to the Lord. "Just set it down," God said. A stool appeared behind him and Abigail placed the bottle there.

The angel looked at the canvas the Father was working on. It was covered in the deepest of purples. A dark navy blue swath blended its way down from the top of the canvas to an absolute black at the bottom.

"Okay," Abigail said. "I give. What is it?"

God said, "Watch." He carefully dipped the edge of the brush so barely a single hair was touching the yellow on his paint pallet. He reached out and gently touched the single dot of yellow into the middle of the dark canvas.

The yellow began to grow. First in a line across the length of the picture. Then the purples seemed to lighten into violets. In turn, each of the dark hues brightened. Before the angel's eyes an immense orange sun rose from the middle of the canvas and turned a black sky to the brightest blue.

God smiled and waved his hand. Immediately the canvas went white again.

"Where did it go?" Abigail asked, sipping her tea.

"Iowa," God said. "They've been having a lot of rain. I thought they might appreciate a nice sunrise. God hung the pallet on a hook attached to the easel, picked up his own tea and sat on the stool.

"Tell me something," Abigail said.

"Anything, my dear," God said, trying to sound like a grandfather.

"You made the sun rise."

"And sent it to Iowa," God repeated.

"No," Abigail said. "I mean you made the sun *rise*. As in "the creation," remember?" She made the little quote marks in the air with her free fingers.

"Oh," God said. "Yes, and the moon too."

"And you saw that they were good."

"That's what it says in the scriptures."

"Right," Abigail said. "Now, was there anything that you saw and said 'Well, that's pretty good' or 'Ya know? I just didn't know where I was going with that one.'"

God took a long drink from his own tea and thought for a moment, then he said, "To answer that question with a *yes* I would have to admit that I made mistakes."

"Not really," said Abigail. "You could say you created things that left room for improvement."

"Well, that I certainly did," God said. "Once I got all the stars in place I had to start on the little things. I'm really more of a big picture guy. I don't do the detail work."

"The detail work," Abigail repeated.

"Sure," said God. "You start things rolling and see where they go. You nudge here and there. You work with it. Then you let it go."

"Okay," Abigail said. "Cows."

"What about cows?"

"Why the udder?"

"So the babies can get milk."

"But you thought up the design. You put the udder there. Why?"

"I had a lot of ideas. Some of them I had to get out of my system before I started on more advanced life forms."

"Like humans," Abigail said.

"Like dolphins," God said. "Dolphins wouldn't have worked with an udder."

"I see," Abigail said. She honestly couldn't tell if the Abba Father was kidding or not. "The neck of the giraffe?"

"Perfect for trees."

"Trees could have been smaller."

"Then all the animals would have eaten them and the giraffes would starve."

"I see," Abigail said again, wondering why she had brought this up. "So humans were...."

"An afterthought," God said.

"An afterthought?"

"I love my animals," God said. "They are all wondrous in each and every way, but I needed someone to take care of them."

"Hence humans," Abigail said.

"Hence humans," God confirmed.

"You told me before you made humans because you were lonely."

"I was," God said. "Can't carry on a conversation with a cow."

"But that was up to you," Abigail said. "They could have spoken if you had wanted them too."

"What would a cow have to say to anybody?" God asked.

"How 'bout 'Jeez your hands are cold!'" Abigail said.

God had just lifted the bottle to his lips when Abigail spoke. He squirted ice tea through his lips and nearly choked. He sputtered and stood up to catch his breath again.

"Sorry," Abigail said, helping God wipe the tea off his smock.

"It's okay," said the Lord. "I set that one up, I guess. You had to say it." He composed himself and sat down on the stool again. "I love the animals. They are my creations. Humans are my children. I love them most of all. That's why I gave them the gift of being able to better themselves. I gave them choice."

"A wolf can choose to find a better cave," Abigail said.

"But a wolf won't choose a cave unless the old one becomes too small or becomes dangerous. Human want to better themselves. They can be hungry and choose not to eat."

"Or most likely, not be hungry and choose to eat," Abigail said. "They can mess themselves up too. Animals won't intentionally choose to be stupid."

"Nobody can make only the right choices," God said. "You can never hope to learn anything if everything you do is right the first time."

"Which brings us back to the beginning," Abigail said. "Were there ever any bad choices or slip-ups on your part that had to be fixed?"

"Have you ever seen a platypus?"

Abigail smiled and nodded her head in agreement.

"Yeah, I don't know what I was thinking on that one," God said. He held out the brush to the angel. "You want to do the moon?"

"Sure," Abigail said. She dipped the brush and began to paint.

Bonus Track

(or whatever the literary version
of a DVD extra is.)

Poker Night

Jesus was bent over, staring into God's refrigerator. "Don't you stock up when you know we're coming over?" the Savior complained.

"What?" God said from the table.

"When you invite guests over to your home it's usually customary to have some food," Jesus said.

"Mi casa es su casa," God said. "You can have your fill of all the food you bring yourself. Bring me an ice tea, please."

"Make it two," St. Peter said. He was sitting to God's left. He usually left the right hand seat open for Jesus. It was a small joke but one that was never lost on the Savior.

"Francis?" Jesus called.

"What's he got in there?" St. Francis yelled toward the kitchen.

"Mostly Snapple," Jesus said.

"Baltic Blast?"

"Two bottles, and one is mine. You want the other?"

"Please," said Francis.

"Are you going to play or be a waiter?" God called.

God and the two saints were sitting around a card table. They were waiting on Jesus, who was still rummaging through the cupboards.

"Ha!" Jesus said. God looked at the ceiling and asked innocently, "Ha, what?"

"You can't hide the good stuff," Jesus called. He entered the room carrying four bottles, two in each hand, and a bag of chocolate chip cookies in his mouth.

"That's gross," St. Peter said. He reached up and grabbed the bag from the Savior's teeth.

Jesus put the bottles down in front of their respective owners and reached over and grabbed St. Peter by the halo. With a snap of his wrist he spun the halo in place. It went round with a "Ziiiinnnnnng" until Peter reached up and stopped it. "You are such a child."

"The only way to get into heaven," Francis said. Jesus smiled. He was going to say the same thing.

"You're the shoe," God said.

"I don't want to be the shoe," Jesus replied. "I wanted to be the top hat."

"Francis is the top hat," Peter said.

"But I was getting food!"

"Snooze you lose," Francis said. Jesus reached over to give Francis' halo a spin, but Francis batted his hand away.

"Can I be the cowboy?" Jesus asked.

"Lost the cowboy," God said.

"How could you lose the cowboy?"

"Gave it to a kid," God said.

The other three stopped and watched the Lord stack his colored money in neat little piles. They waited. God looked up and saw them watching him. "What?"

"There's a story here," Francis said. Jesus opened his Snapple and leaned back in his chair.

"Well," God said. "There was this little girl named Erin. She was playing with the game, even though her mother had said not to, and she lost the cowboy. So she prayed that I would help her before her folks got the game out again."

"You gave away the cowboy?" Jesus asked. "What if we want to play a game with six people someday?"

"We'll use a button or something."

"You'd do that, wouldn't you?" Jesus asked. "You, who could make a real horse run through this room, you'd go and use a button."

"Wouldn't want a real horse on the board," Francis said. "Be too big."

"He could make it really little," Peter said. He was starting to chuckle.

Francis picked up on the line and said, "It might leave something for the little shoe to step in."

Peter laughed out loud. "We never had that problem with the dog."

"The dog is trained well," Francis said. The two men started to giggle at their own humor. Jesus just looked at them. He reached into the box and traded the shoe for a thimble. God continued to stack his money.

Peter picked up the dice and rolled a seven. "What's the rule on prayers?" he asked as he moved his piece along.

"What do you mean?" God asked.

"I mean Francis here gets prayed to all the time," Peter said. "I get them; so does Jess. Some we can answer, some we can't, but *you* get more than the rest of us put together. What's the rule on who gets answers and who doesn't?"

"All prayers get answers." He rolled double fives. "Sometimes the answer is no."

"But how do you decide?" Pete asked.

"Depends," said God. "Depends on who's praying and what they really need at the time."

Francis picked up the dice and rolled a four. God continued. "Little girl who asked for the piece thought her father might hit her if he found out."

"Would he?" Jesus asked.

"Probably," God said. "I gave her the horse from my box and now she has a stronger faith. When she gets older she'll think her mom found it and put it back, but for right now, she truly believes that prayers get answered. She's going to need that."

Jesus rolled a 7 and moved to *Chance*. He drew a card and then looked at his father. "It says, 'You will get your father another ice tea.'"

"Excellent," God said. "When did they add that card to the series?"

"Cut that out," Jesus said. Peter and Francis started to giggle again. Jesus drew another card. It said, "And pass me the cookies."

God had been trying to hold back a laugh and now let it out with a snorting sound. Peter started to shake and had to put his bottle down. Francis was laughing so hard there were tears in his eyes.

"We should make up a card that says 'Stop hitting your child or I'll send you to hell," Jesus said.

He stood and tossed the bag of cookies to his Father as he went to the kitchen.

"That would be spooky," Francis said.

Jesus returned and handed his Father the tea. He sat down and drew another card. This one simply said, "Thanks." Jesus flicked it at the Lord. "Stop it!"

Francis squirted Snapple through his nose and had to leave the table. Peter nearly fell off his chair.

"You know, this never happens when we play with Gabriel," Jesus said.

God chuckled.

(Elsewhere....)

Erin sat across from her father as they played the game. Her father was ahead. As usual. Her mother was barely trying and her brother had left the table when his favorite TV show came on. Martin rolled double sixes and moved the cowboy piece along the board. "9..10..11..12 *Chance*," Martin said. He drew an orange card and read it to himself. The color drained out of his cheeks. He looked like he had the wind knocked out of him. "What the hell is this?" he said, flicking the card at his wife. She picked it up, confused.

"It says 'Go to jail,' Honey. That's all. What's wrong with you?"

Martin took the card from her and read it again. He slid the card under the pile and moved the cowboy to the jail and didn't say a word the rest of the game.

Erin won.

www.ingramcontent.com/pod-product-compliance
Lightning Source LLC
Chambersburg PA
CBHW030256270626
47156CB00022B/2846